# HIGH SKIES

# *HIGH SKIES*

*a novella*

## Tracy Daugherty

2018
Red Hen Press
NOVELLA
AWARD

Red Hen Press | *Pasadena, CA*

Book design by Mark E. Cull

Library of Congress Cataloging-in-Publication Data
Names: Daugherty, Tracy, author.
Title: High skies : a novella / Tracy Daugherty.
Description: First edition. | Pasadena, CA : Red Hen Press, [2021]
Identifiers: LCCN 2020002091 (print) | LCCN 2020002092 (ebook) | ISBN 9781597094450 (trade paperback) | ISBN 9781597098823 (ebook)
Subjects: LCSH: Domestic fiction.
Classification: LCC PS3554.A85 H54 2020 (print) | LCC PS3554.A85 (ebook) | DDC 813/.54—dc23
LC record available at https://lccn.loc.gov/2020002091

Publication of this book has been made possible in part through the financial support of Nancy Boutin.

The National Endowment for the Arts, the Los Angeles County Arts Commission, the Ahmanson Foundation, the Dwight Stuart Youth Fund, the Max Factor Family Foundation, the Pasadena Tournament of Roses Foundation, the Pasadena Arts & Culture Commission and the City of Pasadena Cultural Affairs Division, the City of Los Angeles Department of Cultural Affairs, the Audrey & Sydney Irmas Charitable Foundation, the Kinder Morgan Foundation, the Meta & George Rosenberg Foundation, the Albert and Elaine Borchard Foundation, the Adams Family Foundation, the Riordan Foundation, Amazon Literary Partnership, and the Mara W. Breech Foundation partially support Red Hen Press.

First Edition
Published by Red Hen Press
www.redhen.org

## ACKNOWLEDGMENTS

For details about Operation Longhorn, I drew upon Michael Marks's "How One Texas Town Fell to Communist Rule in the 1950s," published in *Texas Standard* on April 12, 2017.

For her enthusiasm and support, I am grateful to Kate Gale and to the team at Red Hen Press: Natasha McClellan, Rebeccah Sanhueza, and Monica Fernandez.

Pat Edmiston lived the story.

Keith Scribner gave the manuscript an invaluable early read.

As ever, Marjorie Sandor made it possible to breathe.

*for Debra*

# HIGH SKIES

"[This place] throws a man face to face with nature stripped of all distracting elements—no mountains, no trees, no beautiful views, though its very simplicity is more than beauty. It overwhelms. To stay here, a man must face himself."

—John Howard Griffin,
*Land of the High Sky*

# 1.

The first dust storm that spring coincided with the onset of my mother's migraines. Early in the morning, that Friday, she grimaced while she stood at the stove scrambling eggs for our breakfast, and a little later while she packed peanut butter sandwiches and apple slices into clunky lunch pails for my sister and me to take to school. By 8:30, when my father was pulling on his suit jacket and preparing to leave for his job at the independent oil and gas outfit he worked for, she was complaining of a shimmering blue aura flitting at the edges of her eyesight, making her nauseous. The sun was too bright through the kitchen window, she said. It blinded her, though the rays were finely filtered through the leaves of the spunky little pecan tree our father had planted in the backyard just last year. She could barely stand. She propped herself upright by hanging on to the greasy corner of the stove. My father dropped his jacket onto a kitchen chair and moved to help her into the bedroom. Neither of my parents were big or tall, but my mother had never looked so bird-like, trembling, curled within the circle of my father's slender arms. She hadn't done her face and hair yet that morning; her cheeks were the color of the milk I'd spilled on the table earlier while fixing my cereal, and her uncombed hair resembled the checkered maze of the crossword puzzle in the newspaper, lines and angles branching off in all directions.

My father settled her into their bed, still warm and unmade from the night before. Bent over her, his arms gyrating swiftly to arrange the pillows and the sheet just so, he echoed the grace of the professional golfers he liked to watch on the weekends on our brand new Crosley television, their bodies in perfect fluid motion to get the ball down the fairway. He closed the yellow curtains on the small window above the bedside bureau. The curtains were gauzy and sheer; a little sunshine still penetrated the square room, casting a creamy wedge of light onto the green cotton quilt at the foot of the bed. My mother closed her eyes, covered her mouth, and turned her head away on the pillow. Dad told me to run to the bathroom, wet a washcloth with warm water, wring it out, and bring it to him. Gently, he placed the washcloth across my mother's eyes.

"Joe, you gotta get the kids to school," she mumbled. The words barely made it out of her mouth, as though something sticky kept her lips from opening fully.

"None of us are going anywhere," Dad said. "Just stay quiet, all right?"

She moaned softly for a few minutes. Her temples were "pounding," she slurred. Dad held her hand. When it seemed she'd fallen asleep, he whispered to my sister and me to sit with her. He'd be right back. He was going to the kitchen to phone Dr. Edwards. I was ten years old, eager each day for opportunities to prove I was a responsible young adult, but now, left to care for my mother, whom I'd never seen remotely stricken, I felt utterly inadequate for the moment. I tried to push my panic into my stomach and squelch it there at the bottom. All this did was force a cramped tension aping hunger. I wished I could tear into my lunchbox and devour everything in it right then and there. My sister was three years younger than I was. If she felt fear, she didn't show it. She sat calmly on the side of the bed humming the Disney theme. Disney was her favorite new show on the one clear channel we got on the Crosley. As sunlight shifted through the curtains, it caught her curly red hair. Her head appeared to spark into flame. My mother groaned and twitched. The washcloth slid down her cheeks, away from her eyes. I tugged the sleeve of my sister's brown plaid dress to move her out of the light, and readjusted the cloth on Mom's face.

My father came back and said the doctor's assistant had informed him we were doing everything properly. When she felt a little better, steady on her feet, we should drive her down to the office. Dr. Edwards would squeeze her in and take a look at her.

"Meantime," Dad said, "I guess you kids have a day off from school."

"You'll have to write notes for us to take to Mr. Seaker," I said. Raymond Seaker was the school's vice principal.

"We'll take care of it later. I'm going to sit here with Mom. Stay around the house and keep the noise down, okay?"

"Can we turn the television on?" Dee Dee asked.

"Keep the sound low."

The big screen crackled. The black-and-white picture jumped crazily for a few seconds—wavy lines like a child's sketch of lightning bolts—then sharpened. A local morning news show was about to sign off. Oil prices were up. High winds forecast. Just another day in late March on the dry flatlands of Midland, Texas. The year was 1957, and the Permian Basin was booming.

My favorite cartoon show, *Heckle and Jeckle*, came on. They were a pair of talking magpies, always wisecracking their way into trouble, Heckle with a Jimmy Durante whine and Jeckle with a "posh British accent," according to my father. My mother couldn't stand them—those "filthy birds are mean," she said—but I cherished their aggression as a model for getting on in the world ("Don't ever let nobody fool ya," Heckle advised). I called Dee Dee "Old Thing," after Jeckle's name for *his* pal, and walked, cocky, around the house jutting out my chest, just as my feathered friends did whenever they cooked up mischief. Their heads—all beak—curved like footballs. Their eyes were stuck to their pates, where a football's seams would be. In my bird-prancing I'd throw my head back and stare at the ceiling, an activity that often resulted in me crashing into my mother's coffee table or a floor lamp, rousing her from the kitchen, yelling, waving a dish towel to shoo me away.

Now, warned by my father to stay quiet, I wondered if my rambunctiousness had accumulated to the point of triggering my mother's collapse. I sat still next to my sister in front of the television, on the deep green living room carpet. I imagined the carpet's edge as a Maginot line I mustn't cross (Mr. Seaker loved to teach the fifth-grade boys war history). I opened my lunch box and bit ravenously into the sandwich, though I'd scarfed down cereal and eggs only half an hour earlier.

Something *thocked* the kitchen window. *Thock.* And again. *Thock-thock.* I stepped off the carpet (as ineffective as the *real* Maginot line) and ran to see the source of the noise. At that same instant I became aware of an unusual odor—not a smell as much as new weight in the air. The scent of sudden coldness. Through the kitchen window I could see the spindly pecan tree whipping about in a gale, the budding pecans like black marbles flying off its limbs, pounding the glass. I'd never seen a sky like the sky I saw. It was brown—the hue of dirty dishwater. I was used to spotting yellow haze billowing above the horizon; sandstorms were frequent in the West Texas desert. But this was different. Darker. The sunlight that had pained my mother less than an hour earlier was rapidly diminishing in brown ocean-swells shading into black hollows straight overhead.

I figured I should run to my room and turn on the humidifier, the way my mother always did whenever an afternoon sandstorm blew in. I had asthma. The humidifier looked like a big round spaghetti pot, except it was made of glass. My mother was convinced the moist steam it dispensed eased my breathing.

My father slipped into the kitchen to get a glass of water. He sang a song about a dust storm. The song's speaker lost his home to the wind and he had to tell his neighbors goodbye, Dad said. He said it was a Woody Guthrie tune. "We used to sing it in Oklahoma, back in the Dust Bowl days." He and my mother had been raised in Cotton County, Oklahoma just north of the Red River across the Texas line. "I thought conditions had changed since then, with people planting so many trees and green lawns, but I guess not."

He pondered his pecan tree, worry-lines creasing his face. The tree swayed raggedly in the yard. Any minute now, its roots would rip from the ground. He shook his head.

"Is Mom better?" I asked.

"A little." Her temples were no longer throbbing. He hoped we could take her to the doctor in an hour or so.

By noon, when we'd lifted my mother onto her feet and she'd managed to slip on a pair of slacks and a blouse, the sky, in the distance, had turned into earth: an unbroken wall of dust. It wasn't raining on us yet, though brown particles swirled through the town's cool air. "Are you breathing okay, hon?" my mother asked me. My chest had, in fact, tightened some, but I didn't want to worry her. "I'm fine," I said.

"I'm so sorry I threw your day out of whack." Her slur was gone.

"It wasn't your fault, Amy," my father said to her. "Now let's see what Dr. Edwards says."

"I guess you're glad to be out of school, though, home watching those filthy birds?"

Actually, I craved school, and she knew it. I was good at it. My study routines were solid and I enjoyed showing my teachers what I knew. I liked spending lunch periods reading comics with my pal Stevie Williston ("Gimp," other students called him because he'd been born with an arthritic hip and had always walked on crutches). And we all adored Mr. Seaker. He'd pace the playground's perimeter during recess, making himself available to us for counseling, coaching, injury inspections, jokes, and an occasional game of tetherball.

It was just as well my mother still hadn't combed her hair: merciless gusts of wind whipped across the driveway, lashing our faces, making it difficult to open the car doors. My father held her tightly so she wouldn't blow over. Her strength was still low.

Tumbleweeds careened between trucks and cars and buses on the streets. Traffic lights swayed like paper streamers, bouncing on soft wires above the intersections.

"Hello, Troy," Dr. Edwards said to me, shaking my hand in his bland, sparsely furnished waiting room. He was a tall man with hairy ears. "How are your lungs? It's getting rough out there. I hope you're staying indoors as much as possible."

"Yes, sir."

He made some small talk with my dad—"I see oil's up over three dollars a barrel now"—and then he said to me, "Okay, let's take a look at your mom." He turned to her. "And how are you feeling, young lady?" She'd set her mouth in an impatient half-smile, as if to say, *Nice of you to finally notice me.*

She followed the doctor and my father down a narrow hallway to an examining room. Dee Dee and I sat on a black leather couch by the reception desk, staring at the posters on the walls listing the symptoms of influenza and whooping cough. "Be sure to wash your hands several times a day, Old Thing," I said to Dee Dee, reading a poster's medical advice. She giggled.

Twenty minutes later, we were all sitting in Dr. Edwards's office surrounded by rows of gleaming golf trophies and pictures of his smiling family (the kids, and even his wife, wore braces on their teeth, which already looked perfect to me). "We don't exactly know what causes migraines," he explained to us, speaking mostly to my father. "There's good reason to think they're related to stress. Have there been any big changes in your family lately?"

"I got promoted at work," Dad said. "District Geologist. We bought a new Oldsmobile, a television . . . all good."

"Congratulations. Even success tends to cause stress, you know, because it brings change, and change requires some adjustments."

"I'd think the sudden drop in air pressure this morning

had more to do with my headache than learning to live with a television," Mom said dryly.

The doctor laughed. "Well, now, my advice, Amy, is just take it easy. Migraines are unpredictable. Sometimes they come in clusters. Aspirin can help a little, but for the most part, you just have to ride them out as you did today. I wish I had more to tell you."

In the car on the way home, Mom wickedly mimicked the doctor: "Just take it easy, young lady!"

"Honey," Dad said. "You'll stir up the pain again."

"Don't start. I'm not a child. I can handle stress."

"Yes, but you don't have to push yourself."

"If I don't push myself, who'll pack the kids' lunches? And why aren't they in school today?"

A tumbleweed slammed into our hood. It looked like a big bird cage full of thorns. In the distance, the sky was blacker than brown. The dust-swells resembled photographs I'd seen in *Life* magazine of mushroom clouds after an atomic blast.

At my father's insistence, and despite my mother's protests, she went back to bed, keeping the curtains closed. Within a minute of her head hitting the pillow, she was out for the rest of the afternoon. My father sat at the kitchen table, catching up on office paperwork. Dee Dee and I resumed our spots in front of the television. The regular programming had been interrupted for local news reports on the storm. These dispatches moved from the obvious—a correspondent babbling about "high winds" and clutching a lamppost on Main Street to keep from blowing over—to the arcane: a meteorologist describing the composition of dust particles as a combination of "aluminosilicate, $SiO_2$ and $CaCO_3$, with organic compounds of inorganic nitrate." Television was still in its infancy, searching for its voice.

Far more useful were my father's explanations. He took a break from his paperwork to watch with us. He weighed in, as an "old rockhound," on what was happening. "All that dark matter you see in the air, it's bare, dry soil from the ground with bits of rocks worn down by the wind over many, many years," he told us. "When huge gusts roll over it, like today, all this loosely held stuff starts to vibrate, and then it saltates—that means it leaps into the air—and then it slams back into the earth, over and over, breaking into smaller bits. The wind picks it up and shoves it forward, using energy from a mix of hot and cold air and electrical charges."

"Like lightning?" I asked.

"Like lightning, yes."

"Does this happen everywhere?" Dee Dee said. "In Russia? Korea?" Names she'd heard on television.

"No. Only in places that don't see much rain," Dad said. "Plus, there's been a lot of bad farming in Texas and Oklahoma. It makes poor ground, creating the conditions for this. We're getting smarter. Things are getting better, but—" He glanced through the kitchen window at his brave little tree, whipsawing toward the zenith and the lawn.

Ultimately, this first storm didn't cause much worry

in Midland proper. Most of the damage occurred on the "wrong side of the tracks," the eastern half of town, separated quite literally by the Southern Pacific Railroad tracks from downtown and the upper and middle class neighborhoods. One day, Mr. Seaker told a bunch of us kids on the playground that "Negro and Mexican" families lived across the tracks, "pursuing their own ways of life." Each group had its own high school, he explained. "The Mexican school was constructed in the 1920s and the Negro facility, Carver High, opened in 1932," he said. "They've been the state football champs in their league almost every year since then."

I remembered this exchange later, when newspaper accounts of the dust storm listed Carver High students as the event's worst victims, suffering "ocular infections" ("That means dirt got in their eyes," Dad told me), "silicosis" ("Trouble breathing, but worse than your asthma"), and one reported case of pneumonia linked directly to swirling dust. A wheat farmer swore that six jackrabbits had suffocated on his land, and five crows had dropped from the sky gasping for air.

Our fifth-grade class was just beginning a study unit on the development of the solar system. Stevie Williston and I were particularly excited about science lessons—both our fathers were petroleum geologists, and we had inherited their curiosity about natural phenomena. One day on the playground I told Mr. Seaker we'd seen pictures of Mars in class. The Red Planet had dust storms exactly like the one we'd experienced. "Oh yes, and much worse, too," he said. "Sometimes Mars's storms circle its entire circumference. And the dust up there is smaller than ours, which creates more static electricity. That makes it stick to stuff."

"If you were a spaceman, dust would stick to your suit?"

"Most definitely."

I knew Mr. Seaker had once dreamed of being a "space-man" (the word "astronaut" was not yet in common use). He'd been a military pilot. My dad had told me, once, that his family had long been active in West Texas aviation and that Mr. Seaker had served in the air force "with distinction." I didn't know what that meant but I heard school parents refer to him, affectionately, as Flyboy. I saw how eagerly they trusted him. No matter what happened, they said—fire or dust storms or a nuclear attack from Russia—Mr. Seaker would safeguard their kids better than anyone they could imagine.

# 2.

Flyboy's reputation as the children's guardian sprang not just from his military service, his affability and general decency, nor solely from the careful attention he brought to his job at school each day; it grew following a notorious incident at the playground one autumn morning. During the early recess period, the first- through third-grade girls were skipping rope, as usual, and playing dodgeball, their plaid dresses flashing in the sun, resembling, at a distance, colorful insect swarms, their laughter like glass bells in the crisp blue air, when loud accordion music came rumbling up the block accompanied by sharply screeching tires. A battered Pontiac, dented front and back, obviously painted many times, revealing patches of yellow, brown, and blue, pulled to a stop at the playground's north edge, its left front tire just topping the curb. From its radio, guitars, accordions, and fiddles screamed through the car's open windows. Happy cries of "Red Rover, Red Rover, let Katie come over!" died away as four long-haired teenaged boys emerged from the seats. Their skin was dark brown. They each wore long-sleeved cotton shirts unbuttoned nearly to their navels (according to the stories passed later from parent to parent, none of whom were anywhere near the playground that day). The boys slouched against the

Pontiac's hood, crossed their arms, and cooed like an acapella boy band, "Hey *chica*! *Chica chica*! Come see our ride!"

Mr. Seaker had been standing near the jungle gym, cautioning the girls to be careful and to be sure to keep their hems pulled down while they climbed the bars. Now, he approached the boys by the car. He was tall and slender, with larger-than-average eyes, ears, and nose, giving his face a bird-like aspect—another reason, perhaps, for the nickname "Flyboy." He could look like a startled owl (when you told him astonishing facts about Martian dust storms) or like a robin rapidly blinking, searching for worms, whenever an urgent task needed tending on the school grounds—as, apparently, was the case now with these unwanted visitors. Mr. Seaker smelled a smoky odor wafting from the car's ashtrays, like rosemary flakes burning on charcoal.

"Can I help you?" he said.

The boys all laughed. "Nah. Just out drivin'," the tallest one said.

"Your tire has jumped the curb and has damaged school property," Mr. Seaker said. "I'll ask you to remove it, please, and I'll add that it's not appropriate for you to loiter here, staring, making lewd comments. These are children."

"Ain't no lewdness, man. It's a free country. Fella can look, *ese*?"

"Why aren't you boys in school?"

"Our school ain't got no books, man. Nothin' to study."

"Still, you shouldn't be—"

"Or desks or chairs, neither."

"I'm asking you to leave. Now."

The boys laughed again.

Mr. Seaker stepped within inches of the driver's face—close enough to distinguish the individual whiskers on his upper lip that had seemed a thin black smudge from a distance. The boy's skin smelled like bacon grease. Mr. Seaker balled his fists. "Now," he repeated.

For a tense minute, the boys shuffled their feet on the sidewalk, apparently considering surrounding him, but then, at a signal from the driver—a brief head-twitch—they hustled back into the car, cackling and cursing in Spanish. The accordion music kicked in again. Smoke rose from the ash trays, nearly pestilential. As the car squealed away, Mr. Seaker shouted, "I'm not going to see you here again! You got that?"

The girls stood, mouths agape, on the playground behind him, dodgeballs (like big red blisters) clutched to their sides, jump ropes coiled in the dirt. That afternoon, they went home and told their mothers and fathers what happened, and Flyboy's legend began. His mornings at school became feasts of chocolate chip cookies and pound cakes, delivered to him directly by grateful mothers. Sometimes, a woman dropping her child off near the playground, spotting Mr. Seaker walking across the open field, would leave her car parked at a crosswalk in the middle of the street, its driver's side door flung open, while she ran to him waving a plate of fudge. At public school board meetings in the evenings, held at the downtown firehouse, Mr. Seaker's hand grew sore from the repeated thankful grips of fathers, praising him for his "brave defense of our children's innocence." That winter, following a concerted campaign by the parents at our school, Mr. Seaker won the city-wide "Administrator of the Year" award.

On the playground, he'd roll his shirt sleeves to his elbows, his long, tanned arms lifting us up to the monkey bars, his smile a guarantee that the rest of the day—in fact, the rest of our lives—would be fine, just fine.

The details of his confrontation with the boys changed in the story's recounting, depending on who was telling it. The boys were always "Messkins"—that never altered: "Thugs from the wrong side of the tracks." In some versions of the tale, Flyboy grabbed the tallest kid's unbuttoned shirt and threatened to beat him to a pulp. Other variations had him issuing his threats in a soft, but unmistakably firm voice, like Humphrey Bogart in *Casablanca*. Some tellers said the "Messkins" had dirty feet, and the feet were bare, leaving a disgusting trail of mud, sweat, and slime on the school's sidewalk. Others said the boys wore high-heeled leather boots, the steel-capped toes spattered with dried blood from the poor victims they'd kicked. Everyone agreed: the one mistake Flyboy made—his one oversight (and, in retrospect, this predicted what lay ahead for our town)—was that he had not taken a water hose and washed off the sidewalk with extra-strength bleach after the boys had left.

It would be many years before I'd know the details of Mr. Seaker's life, but one day I'd learn that his family had been instrumental in founding what eventually became Webb Air Force Base in Big Spring, a small town forty miles north of Midland, home of a Gulf Oil refinery and a New York Southern Railroad station. The "spring" in Big Spring, once an oasis fiercely fought over by Comanches and Pawnees, had dried up with the discovery of oil and the coming of the railroad in 1925. In the nineteenth century, the Seakers were buffalo hunters and cotton farmers. They owned 225 acres of land that would seed the airport shortly after the Wright brothers made international headlines, and would clear the way for Texas Highway 1, blazing a path for the shiny new Interstate 80. Mr. Seaker's grandfather had ridden in a hot air balloon at the 1893 Chicago World's Fair. He caught the fancy for air travel. Later, back in Texas, he partnered with other ranchers to consolidate land holdings and pave runways in the desert using blades from industrial washers and dryers purchased from a local laundry operator. As an oil hub, Big Spring had no trouble drawing travelers just as soon as the Chamber of Commerce convinced Fokker Universal to inaugurate air service. Soon, Ford Tri-Motors and Lockheed Speedsters lined the runways, wings gleaming, fanning up dust. The US Weather Bureau moved in, hacked away sagebrush and prairie dogs, and built a small office on the site.

Mr. Seaker's father was one of the first men to use the airstrip. One morning he strapped a horse saddle behind the cockpit, in front of the fuselage of a brand new Fokker Super, and flew proud circles over his cotton fields. At one point, a gust of wind caused the plane to dip; his ten-gallon cowboy hat tugged sharply backwards, and the chin strap nearly choked him.

Eleanor Roosevelt, Knute Rockne, Will Rogers, and Harry S. Truman all flew through Big Spring on national tours. In later years, the Chamber of Commerce dropped the names Rockne and Rogers from the airfield's list of famous visitors, after the men died horribly in plane crashes.

During World War II, the airstrip became the Big Spring Army Airfield, home of the 818th Bomber Training Squadron. It was one of the few bases where cadets could learn to use the top-secret Norden bombsight, lauded by the military for its accuracy in pinpointing ground targets. In the mid-forties, AT-11 trainer planes dropped over twelve million one-hundred-pound practice bombs into West Texas sump pits.

A few years later, on his eighteenth birthday, Mr. Seaker joined the military. An advanced Air Training Wing had moved to Big Spring. The field was renamed Webb Air Force Base after Lt. James L. Webb, a West Texas native and combat pilot killed off the Japanese coast in 1949. Mr. Seaker trained in T-28s, using the Norden bombsight, both in Big Spring and at Goodfellow Field in San Angelo, a few miles to the west. The Korean conflict, threats of nuclear war, and fears of communism kept Texans on edge, and activity at high alert on the air bases.

In April 1952, Mr. Seaker participated in a major military training exercise. Operation Longhorn, it was called. In the tiny town of Lampasas, 260 miles west of Midland, the five thousand or so citizens awoke one day to a radio broadcast on the local station, KHIT: "Shortly after eight o'clock this morning, the Aggressor government took control of the city. In rapid order, banks, places of worship, and schools were closed. City officials were arrested and taken to places of confinement. The court system will be downsized to a single magistrate. Dissent will be punishable by death."

That morning's paper, the *Lampasas Dispatch*, a special edition, announced that Texas had been conquered by the "Aggressor Nation," a malevolent military force swarming in from Central Europe, following an atomic blast in nearby Corpus Christi. Other regions of America had fallen, the paper reported matter-of-factly. Florida. New England.

In the courthouse square, people gathered to hear the city manager announce, "All we can do under the circumstances is to passively resist until we are liberated by our own US forces."

The bank president grabbed the microphone from him and spoke against the invasion. Two "Aggressor" MPs hauled him off to jail. Meanwhile, on the radio, a woman having identified herself as "Aggressor Annie" broadcasted seductive propaganda messages: "Hello, boys. We are not really enemies, but friends. Let's get together."

These activities were all part of an elaborate war game,

the largest ever held at that time in the United States. The object was to train soldiers to respond in the event of a hostile occupation within US borders. One hundred fifteen thousand men engaged in the exercise. Most of the "invaders" were members of the American 82nd Airborne Division. Mr. Seaker's job was to impersonate an Aggressor communications minister. His picture appeared on the newspaper's front page, above the caption, "We are at war with the United States army and its generals, who are nothing more than political gangsters." The paper bore the date "Juvember 33, 1969," next to big block letters making it clear that this edition had been printed for "MANUEVER PURPOSES ONLY." This was in case unsuspecting readers, who'd somehow failed to be alerted to the exercises, were tempted to believe the news.

The planners had a sense of humor: Mr. Seaker was dubbed "Regimentestro (Colonel) Alton M. Schiepstock." He issued a statement: "With the unfurling of the Aggressor flag at the county courthouse this morning, we extend the hand of friendship to the people of Texas. No longer will you be shackled by the bonds which the filthy, capitalistic Wall Street warmongers have used to enslave you since 1845. Long live the glorious Aggressor Nation."

By the evening of April 3, hundreds of tanks had spread across a sixty-by-thirty-mile area west of Waco, hundreds of paratroopers had parachuted onto the highways, and the liberation of Lampasas had begun. In some scenarios, the army used real ordnance; a live hand grenade, buried in the ground, would be unearthed by school children three decades later, at around the time I learned about this period in Mr. Seaker's life. Three soldiers died when their parachutes failed to open. Seven others perished, accidentally, in the "fake" fighting. By the time the maneuvers came to an end, most of the local ranchers, who had agreed in advance to lend their land to the army, complained bitterly about trampled crops and broken fences. Townspeople admitted it had been "all too real, too scary" to see their banker carted off to prison, and to listen to the radio propaganda. They sorely regretted allowing Lampasas to be sacrificed as Ground Zero in what the *Dispatch* called a "war to control the world."

Mr. Seaker returned to Webb Air Force Base to serve out his time in the military. By then, his brother Paul, two years younger, was also training there, flying the brand new T-33s.

On his days off at Goodfellow Field, while he was stationed in San Angelo, Mr. Seaker walked regularly into town. He'd catch a Frank Sinatra movie at the cinema, grab a soda at the Rexall's, or sit in a downtown park with a transistor radio in his lap, listening to Stan Kenton on KGKL. The necklaces and rings in the windows of Holland's, a corner jewelry store, always caught his eye as he passed, and he wished he had a special someone to buy nice things for. Then one day, as he stood at the window, he glanced past the jewelry on display to the front counter inside the store.

The sales clerk, a slim blonde woman wearing a red print dress, was smiling at him. He smiled back. Then, bashful and flushed, he hurried on back to base.

At the time, Goodfellow Field housed a number of men suffering what the military then called "combat fatigue"—pilots who'd patrolled the skies over Europe during the war and who "required more time to adapt again to flying," according to official statements in the base newspaper. Mr. Seaker saw the truth: they were scared to death. They'd survived being strafed during dogfights, barely escaped their burning planes, and now they were willing to forego their pay and risk court martial rather than continue serving.

Spooked by the thought that he could wind up just like them, he reconsidered his decision to re-enlist. He urged himself back to the jewelry store one day with the conscious intention of testing a different future. He would speak to the woman in the red dress.

Her name was Mary Louise Thompson. Mr. Seaker learned little about her during that first brief chat (the store happened to be quite busy that day) but she told him she loved Frank Sinatra, and that prompted their first date at the cinema the following Saturday afternoon.

Her father was a school administrator in San Angelo. In addition to working at the jewelry store, she taught third-graders part-time as a teacher's assistant. One day, on R&R from the base, Mr. Seaker dropped by her school while her class was at recess. She wore a blue dress that morning, and he was happy to see she looked splendid no matter what color she chose to display. She had the slightly chubby face of cherubs in Sunday School lesson books, and short, slender legs that—by contrast—made her arms look longer than they were. She laughed as Mr. Seaker, sleek in his khaki military garb, ran around the softball diamond with her students. "You're really good with kids," she said to him later that day, as they sat at the Rexall's soda counter sharing a banana float. He'd never given a thought, of any kind, to children, and her words struck him as a revelation. In meeting Mary Louise, he had discovered more than *one* future.

Within six weeks, at the time of his discharge, he was back at the jewelry store buying a ring for her. Her father, a kindly man who took to Mr. Seaker right away, and was the first to call him "Flyboy," contacted teachers at a San Angelo junior college, and set Mr. Seaker on the path toward a degree in elementary education.

He and Mary Louise were married to the strains of an Irish reel, "The Glass Island," Irish folk music being her other great passion, along with Frank Sinatra. Her grandmother had told her once that the family came from Donegal, many generations ago. Mary Louise would listen to the music on a phonograph and dream of flying someday to Ireland. Her father—a man with an inordinate fondness for nicknames—called her "Slipjig," after her favorite dance rhythm. "Here's to Slipjig and Flyboy," he toasted them at the wedding. "Together, may they soar."

Mr. Preston, the principal at our school in Midland, appreciated what he saw the first time he met "Flyboy" Seaker, and made him an offer on the spot, at the interview for the position of vice principal in the spring of 1954. He didn't even consider other candidates. Mr. Seaker hesitated only because, at the time, the school had no available teaching positions for Mary Louise. She reasoned that she would soon want children, so perhaps it was best that she not seek work right away. Mr. Seaker started his job in the fall of 1955. Following the incident with the "Messkins" from the "other side of the tracks," Mr. Preston was never happier with his decision to hire the personable young veteran.

By August 18, 1955, shortly after the US Supreme Court's *Brown v. Board of Education* decision, and coinciding, roughly, with Mr. Seaker's one-year anniversary as vice principal, twenty-eight Texas schools had drafted plans for complete or partial desegregation. These schools were in some of the state's larger cities: San Antonio, Austin, Corpus Christi. In the smaller towns, like Midland, the US Supreme Court had never really existed.

It wouldn't be until 1968 that the Midland Independent School District would bus white kids across town to what had traditionally been "minority" schools in an effort to eliminate racial discrimination. The busing commenced only after the United States government filed a lawsuit against Midland for not complying with *Brown v. Board of Education*. The school district argued it could not be held responsible for the "myriad factors of human existence which can cause discrimination in a multitude of ways on racial, religious, or ethnic grounds." It was a "familiar phenomenon that in metropolitan areas minority groups are often found concentrated in one part of the city. In some circumstances certain schools may remain all or largely of one race because of housing patterns." Once again, this was not the school district's concern, argued Midland's lawyers. The United States disagreed.

My sister was among the first students to be bused. "I don't see why *your* education should be watered down in these poor schools just because the Mexicans and blacks choose to live in one part of town," our father groused.

"Maybe they don't *choose* to live there," Dee Dee said. "And their schools aren't equal to those in this part of town." She'd heard these words on the television news.

"Why is that *our* problem?" Dad said.

But that was 1968. In '57, the year of the dust storms, the desegregation of Midland schools was still a long way off— except in one peculiar case, for which, rightly or wrongly, the legendary Flyboy, Mr. Preston's right-hand man, would be credited. Or blamed.

# 3.

The south side of our school playground was lined with three large Quonset huts, round, rectangular structures made of wood and aluminum siding, resembling small airplane hangars. They had been built in the 1940s, when US troops were first deployed in Europe, and bombardier training ramped up in Big Spring. So many cadets disembarked at the railway station in such a short time, base housing ran out, and Quonset huts were erected overnight all over West Texas. For the duration of the war, soldiers slept at our school—on strict orders not to interfere with the children—bused daily up to Big Spring and back for their training exercises.

The army shuttered the huts the day the bombs dropped on Nagasaki. Cobwebs accumulated in their musty interiors. Sheets of dust, twigs, and cottonwood fuzz filtered into the buildings through cracks in the windows. For years, at school board meetings every month, our principal Mr. Preston complained that the huts were not only a nuisance and a waste of space, but they were dangerous as well. A vast amount of staff vigilance was required to keep children from cutting their hands on the walls' fraying aluminum trim or from stepping on broken glass. He urged the district to either tear down the structures or find new uses for them.

In early April, that spring of 1957, two weeks before the second dust storm blew into the basin, Mr. Preston announced at a board meeting that recently he had formulated exciting new plans for the Quonset huts, as yet undetailed, and he asked the board's permission to pursue feasibility studies. He requested that further discussions of his proposal be conducted in closed sessions.

Mr. Preston is the person I know least about in this story. As a child, I had no reason for curiosity concerning him, other than learning how not to perturb him during the school day. In later years, I found no occasion to think about him—until I began to recall the year of the dust storms and to wonder what had really happened to all of us, and why, in that strange, brown-tinted period.

Even as a kid, I had heard it said that Mr. Preston was a rare political "progressive" in Midland (without any clue as to what that meant). I had also heard him spoken of as an "opportunist, willing to toe the establishment line, looking for a promotion and a ticket out of Texas." Whatever the case—and however responsible he may have been for triggering the events that spring—because he'd announced that he was putting his vice principal in charge of "building use," what later occurred fell squarely at Mr. Seaker's feet.

The storm blew in on a Monday afternoon. It was as though the earth tilted: the ground seemed to advance toward us relentlessly at a ninety-degree angle. What little remained of the sky was nearly obscured in a thin wedge on the western horizon, a dim blue—almost purple—backdrop to the skeletal outlines of oil rigs and windmills surrounding our town.

I was on the playground when the first gusts stirred dust devils at my feet. I ran toward the classroom buildings, dodging a minefield of little tornadoes. Immediately, my chest tightened and each breath felt like a fist slamming my ribs. The air smelled of sewage—we later learned that several pipes had broken and septic tanks had ruptured on the "other side of the tracks." Cattle waste had also been sucked up and spread by the winds. In the time it took me to sprint from the center of the open field to my classroom door, the air temperature plummeted over ten degrees—almost icy. Our teacher told us that a sudden cold front had slammed into the region, powered by rain-cooled air generated from a thunderstorm brewing miles away. The cooler air had hit a dry air mass over Midland, creating "convective instability"—"All those gusts you're experiencing," the teacher explained. He wanted us to know exactly what we were looking at: "The winds move in directions opposite to the way the thunderstorm is traveling, and they move *into* the storm. When the storm collapses, all those breezes racing around inside it reverse course, and shoot outward, pushing forward that big wall of dust you're seeing out the window right now."

Mr. Seaker poked his head into the doorway and told me

I had a phone call in the principal's office. It was Dad. Over the scratchy line he heard my rattling wheeze. "Sit tight. I'll try to leave work early this afternoon and get you home to the humidifier. Your mom's gone to bed with another headache. Check on Dee Dee if you get a chance, okay? I'll see you as soon as I can."

Dee Dee's class, the second-graders, was glued to the big, smudged windows in its room, each kid cradling a box of Crayons, drawing the storm—a scramble of brown scribbles. Dee Dee seemed safe and content for now. As I walked down an open-air corridor, back to my own room, blasts of stinging particles buffeted me against the brick wall. A tea-kettle whistling filled the air. Dust song, I thought.

In class, we spent the early afternoon reviewing the history of drought in Texas, after Stevie Williston asked, "It's drought that feeds these storms, right?" He'd heard his dad say as much at the dinner table. The teacher agreed. He pulled a reference book from a shelf behind his desk. In 1822, he said, flipping pages, the first colonists in Texas, under the leadership of Stephen F. Austin, saw their food crops die from lack of moisture. In 1908, a man named C. W. Post, of Post Toasties fame, spent over fifty thousand dollars on explosives to try to blow rainwater out of the sky, above the Texas Panhandle. He bragged he could "shoot up a rain whenever he wanted to," but he failed, repeatedly, and then came the "dirty thirties," the Dust Bowl days, with drought covering over one hundred million acres in Texas and Oklahoma. "The soil was dry to a depth of three feet," our teacher read. Sometimes, when the air cooled suddenly, the atmosphere was so full of electricity, the rising dirt would come to a cold boil.

By this time, my breathing had grown so labored, my teacher became concerned. He rummaged around in the janitor's closet at the back of the classroom. He found a gauze mask for me to wear. We moved on, then, to a discussion of the solar system. "Mars's atmosphere is about one percent as dense as the Earth's," the teacher read to us. "To fly a kite on Mars, the wind would need to be much faster than on Earth to even lift the kite off the ground." No one paid any attention to him. The kids had all turned in their seats. They were staring at me in my mask sitting next to Stevie. His crutches were stacked at his feet. "Gasper and the Gimp," someone whispered.

Dad arrived at around 2:30 p.m. in the Oldsmobile. He took me and Dee Dee home. We tiptoed into the darkened bedroom to check on my mother. She was sleeping, a damp cloth hiding her eyes. Dad set up the humidifier, and told me to lie down. I heard *Heckle and Jeckle* in the living room—Dee Dee had turned on the television. Though I sorely missed the birds, the steam-hiss from my "spaghetti pot" lulled me to sleep. Hours later, my breathing had calmed. When I woke, I saw that Dad had placed wet rags along the window sills in the kitchen. The pecan tree was bowed but standing. Mom was on her feet, feeling better.

The next day, Dr. Edwards checked us both. He prescribed an inhaler for me, "to use only in dire emergencies.

They're predicting more of these storms in the next few weeks. I hate to restrict your activities, Troy, but it's best if you stay indoors. Catch up on your homework, eh?"

"I *am* caught up."

"Well, you know what I mean."

He turned to my mother. "Now, as for you, young lady, I have no hesitation restricting *you*. It's all well and good to be a successful homemaker, like the women in those magazines—" Sitting next to her, I felt my mother's arms tense, and I was convinced her head was going to throb. The only time she *saw* "those magazines," *Harper's Bazaar*, *Ladies Home Journal*, was in Dr. Edwards's waiting room. "—but you can't do it all, Amy. Stress will absolutely debilitate you if you don't take it easy." He suggested she hire a personal shopper to get her groceries, and maybe a part-time housekeeper.

"Who the heck does he think I am?" she exploded at my father once we reached home. "The Queen of the Desert? We can't afford a housekeeper!"

"No, we can't," my father admitted. "But the kids can help you more around the house. I can do more of the shopping."

"That would be lovely, Joe. But that's not the point. The point is, I'm not a wilting flower, fading at the first touch of stress. I'm not helpless. I'm a grown woman. Our good doctor doesn't seem to understand the first thing about grown women. *He's* been reading too many silly magazines. Maybe we should find another physician."

"Honey, he knows the kids, their histories. We can't just—"

"Why not?"

"And these headaches of yours, they're—"

She patted my chest. "My headaches are just like his breathing. We live in a harsh place. It triggers—"

"Oh. So it's *my* fault?"

"What? No . . ."

"I brought us here. For my job. If I weren't out looking for oil, then you and Troy would be the picture of health?"

"No, no. Joe. I didn't say that. I just meant—"

"I know what you meant." He turned abruptly, and pushed open the back door. He went to check on his pecan tree. As he was propping the tree upright, tying its thin trunk to wooden stakes in the lawn, Mom retreated to her bedroom. The curtains remained closed. I followed her quietly. "Does your head hurt?" I asked.

"No, sweetie. I'm fine. Just tired. I think we're *all* tired of this blowing dust. I'll be up in a minute to make your supper, okay?"

Even with the stakes, our pecan tree drooped more than it had, its limbs curled as if it was trying to twist into the letter *S*.

As with the first storm, this second event did most of its damage across the tracks. In our part of town, the worst disruption occurred at San Jacinto Junior High. Spring football practice had to be canceled when most of the offensive line, during a scrimmage drill, fell over coughing in a grassy heap. Two of the players missed several days of school after that, suffering dust inhalation and severe dehydration.

To the east of the Southern Pacific rails, residents reported seeing "brown snow." Streetlights on Cotton Flat Road snapped on at noon, and then disappeared in thick black clouds. The "duster" ruined thousands of dollars of wheat. "I just sat there and watched my farm move on down the highway," said one elderly rancher.

Once again, the students at Carver High took a terrible hit. A sophomore girl whose symptoms of "dry eye" went untreated for three days woke up blind one morning, according to the *Midland Reporter-Telegram*. Sixteen cases of "dust pneumonia" were recorded, three of them severe, requiring round-the-clock observation in the intensive care unit. "Virus spores and toxic aerosols are more common in lower-income neighborhoods," explained one local official from the US Weather Bureau. "Minute dust particles become carriers of these elements. Like honeybees spreading pollen, they distribute them over a vast range." Of further concern was the scarcity of medical facilities in east Midland, he said, and the tendency of "under-educated families" to hew to superstitions, attributing serious signs of disease to "stretches," "fits," or "just a little griping in the stomach." A surprising number of unsanitary outdoor privies remained extant in that part of town, despite modern advances in plumbing.

Midland Memorial Hospital reported one case of pellagra, following the storm. "Pellagra?" my father said, dropping the paper on the kitchen table one morning at breakfast. He sipped his coffee. "Dust didn't cause *that*," he said. "That's an Okie disease—used to see it all the time, among the tenant farmers' kids. Their skin'd get all scaly and crusty—"

"Joe! The children are trying to eat their cereal!" Mom called from the stove.

"It's malnutrition, that's all it is," he finished quietly. "Those people ought to feed their kids."

My breathing was better, but three days after the storm I still had a wheeze, so Mom slipped my inhaler into my back pocket as I left for school. On the playground, Mr. Seaker warned me not to overexert. I sat on the sidelines next to Stevie while the other kids played softball, skipped rope, or ran around a small obstacle course. The course consisted of dry gullies to leap across, a pair of wooden walls to scale, and steel poles to swing around on your way to the next challenge. "Gasper and the Gimp!" kids shouted at us—the outcasts—while they did the things healthy children do. They figured they'd live forever.

We're not Gasper and the Gimp, I thought. We're Heckle and Jeckle, the smart-talkers, the sneaks, one step ahead of everyone else. We'll show *them*! Stevie had, in fact, perfected the art of insulting his peers without them even realizing he was mocking them. He'd learned never to respond directly to ridicule. He was too frail to defend himself if confrontations turned physical. When someone said to him, "Out of my way, Gimp," he'd say nothing, wait a day or two, and then approach the offender—at lunch, perhaps—offering something like, "Maybe you can help me with a history report. Do you know where the anal canal is?"

"I dunno. Africa? Egypt?"

Stevie would stare dryly at his tormentor and nod.

One day, when Mr. Seaker had been called away from the field for a telephone call in his office, when no one was watching, Stevie and I took a tube of Elmer's Glue from our classroom. We slathered the stuff all over the steel poles on the obstacle course. About twenty minutes later, when our classmates made their turns on the course, they stopped in their tracks and picked at the sticky film smearing their fingers. "Ewww!" "Gross!" "What *is* this?"

With a show of great indifference, Stevie and I moved away from the scene of the crime, victorious against our enemies: "Don't never let *nobody* fool ya!" If a person could high-step with crutches, Stevie did just that.

We approached the Quonset huts. Someone had cleared the shattered glass that used to glimmer in the dirt near the buildings' doors—either that or the last storm had blown it all away. No: the old cracked panes had been replaced. Someone had removed the worst of the jagged aluminum edge peeling back from the hut's main frame. Curious, I asked Stevie to prop a crutch against one of the structure's gently curved sides. I used the crutch to boost myself to a window. Squinting, I peered inside. Staring back at me was a round black face, eyes wide, mouth open in amazement. I gave a startled scream. I heard a scream inside the hut. The figure fell away from the glass, just as I toppled backwards off Stevie's crutch, raising a cloud of dust.

# 4.

The first time I saw Stevie's crutches, in the lunch room, in first grade, I wanted to run away from him. Naturally, the fact that he was different frightened me. And the crutches meant he had a disease. I didn't want to catch whatever afflicted his body. It took many weeks for me to feel comfortable around him—weeks of closeness (teachers sat us together at lunch one day and the arrangement stuck), of talking to him, of learning we liked science and the same comic books. My mother had told me he suffered from arthritis—it wasn't a "communicable" disease, she said.

Even as a child, I was struck by the implications of her wording: if you communicated, you got sick. On the other hand, sickness also spread from lack of communication—a circumstance our community soon endured.

On September 4, 1957, Texans would watch on television as National Guardsmen in the neighboring state of Arkansas, on orders from Governor Orval Faubus, blocked nine black students from entering Central High School in Little Rock, while a growing crowd chanted, "Go home!" Texans weren't the only ones watching. Immediately, all over the world, the Soviet Union disseminated press releases mocking American rhetoric about freedom and equality in the face of such obvious racial discrimination. School segregation became a major Cold War issue—a weapon in the global conflict. Months earlier, in the spring, at the time of the storms, our hardscrabble town had engaged in Cold War combat, and our schools played a role in the drama.

Because of its proximity to Webb Air Force Base, Midland became awash in rumors, in mid-April, concerning a Soviet installation in the Southern Ural Mountains. US intelligence had gathered information about an incident there, in the Chelyabinsk district: stories of ugly, purplish skies, rich farmland plowed under overnight, livestock slaughtered. The Soviet government offered no official statements, and managed to successfully impose a news blackout, but some of the men stationed at Webb knew that Chelyabinsk was the home of the Mayak nuclear facility. In 1949, it had produced the Soviet Union's first atomic bomb. These men knew that, in addition to the ruined farmland and murdered cattle, villagers downstream from Mayak were reporting dozens of cases of radiation sickness. These men, the important men who knew all this—they became a little too relaxed in the evenings while on R&R from Webb, a little too lubricated. They talked about Mayak. Word got around Big Spring. It made its way to Midland. One day at work my father heard about Mayak from a colleague, who'd got it from a friend of a friend who knew a colonel at Webb. There had been an accident, releasing radiation. It had happened because Soviet officials were putting enormous pressure on the facility to build more bombs. Clearly, the communists were gearing up for large-scale war.

Midland, Texas in 1957 was not the only mid-American town paranoid about communism and the possibility of a nuclear attack. Nor was it the only town with a conservative city council whose members prided themselves on patriotism, men (for they *were* all men) who considered Senator Joseph R. McCarthy a role model (he had died that spring of alcohol-related causes). The Senator's work, of rooting out communist spies wherever they infected American institutions, would not die with him, these men insisted.

Midland, Texas was not the only place in 1957 whose city council wanted to "send a patriotic message" (*to whom* was not entirely clear), a warning about the escalating arms race. It was not the only place to pass an official ordinance forbidding visits from persons traveling to the United States on Soviet passports, as well as citizens from Eastern Bloc countries. Such ordinances went into effect that year on Long Island, in northern California, and in most of the mid-sized towns along the east coast of Florida.

Midland's councilmen cited the town's oil production, crucial to the nation's future energy needs, and its location near Webb Air Force Base as the primary reason to ban Soviets from traveling to the region—who knew what military secrets they might try to steal? But it was also the case that, in the wake of *Brown v. Board of Education*, these same places, towns like Midland proudly making strong Cold War stances, were strenuously fighting federal efforts to integrate their public schools. Even before the events in Little Rock, Arkansas, it was national news that the Soviet Union regularly tried to embarrass the United States on the world stage by playing up racial strife in its cities. Even my father, who said he supported the Midland City Council's stand against communism, mused aloud one day, "Maybe they don't want the Russkies here because they don't want them to see what it's like on the wrong side of the tracks."

By May 1, "Mayak" had become such a familiar word in Midland, our teacher invoked it during our regularly-scheduled "Duck and Cover" drill. We scrambled under our desks—me after helping Stevie move his crutches and bend to the floor, gently, without exacerbating the pain in his hip. We covered our heads with our arms, our prescribed pose for surviving a nuclear attack. We each received, from the teacher, a set of military-style dog tags with our names and addresses printed on them, so we could be identified in the chaos following an atomic blast. The tags also included our official religion, so we'd be buried in the proper cemetery in case our parents didn't survive to supervise the arrangements.

As we crouched beneath our desks, the teacher said, "This might be a good time to say the Pledge of Allegiance again, to remind ourselves how lucky we are to live in this country, and how diligent we must be to protect our freedoms." On our knees, on the hard linoleum floor smelling of lemon wax, we all twisted to face the small American flag in the front of the room, displayed above the chalkboard.

The drill occurred two weeks after I had glimpsed the black face through the window of the Quonset hut on the playground. Besides Stevie, I didn't tell anybody what I'd seen for a couple of days. But then I mentioned it to my mom. She didn't seem to fully grasp what I was saying. "Hm. That's odd," she said distractedly. Then she sliced an apple for my lunch. I forgot about the incident.

One morning, a few days later at the breakfast table, my father said a friend of his who sat on the school board told him that Mr. Preston had apparently made a deal with Carver High School. Carver classrooms had been damaged in the dust storms. The repairs would take time, and space was at a premium. With school board approval, Mr. Preston ordered city workers to clear out one of the Quonset huts, make sure it conformed to the city's safety codes, and received an upgrade in electrical wiring. He offered the space to a couple of teachers from Carver and to a handful of their students until the "Negro" buildings could be fixed.

My mother set a plate of eggs on the table. "That sounds like . . . wait." She turned to me. "Didn't you say . . . what were you telling me the other day?"

I repeated my story about Stevie's crutch and the window and the startled black face I'd seen.

"I guess it's happening, then," Dad said.

My mother touched my shoulder. "Honey, you should keep your distance from that hut, okay?"

"I'm not surprised they're keeping it quiet," Dad said. "Melvin"—his friend on the school board—"said fellows were split on the plan. It received majority approval, and it's good for *our* school because the district is funneling added funding this way to accommodate the extra students. But some of the board members thought this was the first step toward integrating all of the city's schools, and they weren't happy with that idea. According to Melvin, one fellow said, 'Preston better decide if he's loyal to the people of Midland or to the federal government.'"

By the time news of the deal *did* make the *Reporter-Telegram*, at the end of the week, that remark about loyalty had been altered and was now directed at Mr. Seaker. Mr. Preston had made it clear to the newspaper reporter that he had put his vice principal in charge of overseeing the plan's implementation.

One of the oil rigs owned by the company my father worked for had suffered minor damage in the dust storms. He was told to drive out and inspect the repairs one day. It was a Saturday, so he wondered if I'd like to come for a ride.

I enjoyed going into the desert with him. The last time we'd done this, he'd opened up, prompted by my questions, about his Oklahoma childhood and his introduction to my mother. "We were in school together, so we'd always known each other," he said. "We spoke seriously for the first time as teenagers, at a powwow in the city park. There were a lot of Comanches and Kiowas in our town, and every summer the Comanches would hold a public dance and a picnic feast. White kids would go to the park, stand at the edge of the field, and watch. That's where I first really got to know your mom."

"Did the Indians care that you were watching them?"

"Not at all. I had a lot of Comanche friends, growing up."

"Did they live in just one part of town?"

"It's a funny thing," Dad said. "Looking back, I guess the schools were segregated. I don't know *where* the Indian kids went to school, to tell you the truth. Not with us. It's not something I thought about at the time. But generally, in town, no, the neighborhoods weren't separate. Families mixed together, house by house, up and down the blocks. I was aware that most of the Indians I knew were poorer than the white folks, and usually their houses and lawns didn't look as nice. But they weren't huddled in a different part of town."

In these conversations, my father wasn't the man he later became—in 1968, say, when my sister was bused to schools across the tracks. By then, he'd become hardened against the concept of integration, specifically against the federal government's "interference"—"Bunch of Washington bureaucrats telling me how I can, and should, educate my children." His impatience with the politics of integration inevitably informed his racial views. "I'm not a racist, but," he'd begin, and then he'd reel off judgments about "Negro" kids' capacities for learning. At that point, I was old enough to know it was fear for my sister—the quality of *her* education—that made him talk like this.

In the late 1950s, during our car trips into the desert, he was a man sincerely grappling with his innate decency, his sense of fairness, his past behaviors. "We'd call them stinkin' Indians," he'd say of the Comanche kids he was raised with. His tone betrayed no belligerence, no self-righteousness. It suggested innocent wonderment. "And then, in the summers, we'd spend all day with them, swimming, fishing, laughing, playing baseball. We were best buddies."

That Saturday in '57, as we made our way to the rig, he talked about his childhood pals. Then he sang a song about a woman in Snyder and her tool-pusher beau who only cared about drilling for oil.

The well, a black tower composed of steel beams criss-crossed like the straps of my sister's bathing suits, stood in stark contrast against the sky, bright blue that day instead of the dark brown it had been most of the last few weeks. The air smelled like rotten eggs. My father said the well's old drill bit, suspended from a cable so it could punch holes in the earth, had been blunted by the dust's scouring force. He examined the new bit, and the temper screw at the base of the worm gear controlling the cable—the gear had been clotted with dirt. "Okay, the cable tension seems good now," he said. The pipeline manifold, a series of snake-like steel tubes regulating oil flow, was secure, and the booster compressor station, providing pressure to push the crude through the pipeline, had been thoroughly cleansed of the "brown snow" that made it stall. "All right. America's energy is on the move again!" my father crowed. Satisfied, he said maybe we could grab some ice cream on the way home.

In the car, I asked him again about the "stinkin' Indians" he had called his pals. "Why did they stink?" I said.

"They didn't. Not really. We said that to insult them—to feel superior, you know? But it was all in good fun. Like giving a buddy a nickname. The white folks in town . . . they'd say the Indians were lazy and drunk all the time. They'd say it with affection about their Kiowa friends. They'd laugh as if they didn't really mean it. But it was also . . . I have to say . . . sort of true." He turned into town off the highway, in the tilting shadow of a billboard advertising "Country Radio." The billboard had been ripped to shreds by the recent storms. "Maybe it was because they couldn't get jobs. Maybe it *was* discrimination, I don't know. But a lot of the time, a lot of Indians *did* just hang around downtown, by the bowling alley and the barber shop, and a lot of them *did* drink too much. The things we'd say . . . the insults, friendly or not . . . they were wrong for lumping all Indians together. But they weren't *all* wrong." He shook his head. In the strain of his voice, I could hear how much he was still at war with himself, even after so many years. "The things I saw on the streets, I didn't always *want* to see. But there it was."

# 5.

The third storm struck on a Wednesday, knocking out electricity for well over three hours in the "good" part of town. When the television came back on, newscasters introduced a fresh term to their audiences—"haboob." "It's an Arabic word," said an excited local weatherman. "You know, the nomads over on the Arabian Peninsula, they've dealt with a few of these storms. 'Haboob' means 'blasting' or 'drifting,' and I'm told the word is often used around the world to describe the kinds of gusts we're experiencing—downbursts of cold air that approach with little warning and create massive walls of sediment. Right now in the Permian Basin winds are steady at forty-two miles per hour, and small-craft pilots have reported impenetrable dust clouds as high as twenty thousand feet. Later today, in addition to the dust, we're likely to experience a mud bath. If the air stays as hot as it is now at lower elevations, then rainfall from this latest thunderstorm"—the weatherman pointed to a map—"this system right here, approaching us from the east, will evaporate before it hits the ground. But all the dust in the cooler air up above will mix with the rain, forming huge mud splatters."

For once, his forecast proved correct. Before the day was out the main thoroughfares downtown had become rivers of twig-spiked mud, blocking sewage drains. Telephone lines snapped all over town, prompting curfew warnings from the police department. Children under sixteen should not be out after dark, said the police chief: dozens of exposed live wires were jumping around like rattlesnakes on the sidewalks.

In my family, the storm's fallout was three-fold: I addressed Dee Dee, "Hey, Boob!" When my mom warned me to cut it out, I answered smartly, in my best magpie voice, "But it's an Arabic word!" My dad bought us a new humidifier, battery-operated so it wouldn't be crippled in the next blackout. And my mother refused to see Dr. Edwards ever again. She'd gone to bed with another migraine six hours before the storm hit town. Vomiting. Slurred words. "Stress is not my problem," she told Dad afterwards. "Clearly, there's a hormonal or chemical surge occurring, some kind of imbalance, whenever the atmosphere changes. When the air pressure drops, or the temperature . . . anyway, I will *not* sit and listen to that ignorant man tell me again how defeated I am by hard work."

"Honey, that's not what he's saying!"

"Joe, if you and the kids want to keep seeing him, fine. But I'm going to look for a *woman* doctor."

Tensions remained high between my folks in the next two weeks as she searched for a female physician—and found one in the town of Odessa, twenty miles away. This doctor, Kimberley Atkins, told my mother she had little patience with the reactionary nature of most of her colleagues in the medical profession. "Disease is better prevented than cured, in my book," she said. "Why wait for it to strike? A good exercise regimen would be useful in your case—because I agree with you that your symptoms are physical, not emotional. The arteries in your brain are somehow constricting, exactly the way your son's lung passages close up whenever he has an asthma attack. You may be right that things like air pressure have an effect." She encouraged my mother to enroll in a beginning modern dance class in Midland, held three times a week, and to practice push-ups and sit-ups every day at home: "Keep the blood flow clear and strong."

Before I'd heard this advice, I think I believed people's lives were set in advance—you were on a path, determined at birth by your mental and physical attributes, and you had no alternative but to follow it. Mr. Seaker had been blessed. Someone like Stevie came up short. *Choice* was not a word I understood.

Now, a different view emerged for me (admittedly, in the form of a sentimental parable my mother might have crocheted on a wall hanging): life rained on you; you could sit and get drenched, or, like Mom, you could seek cover.

But the rain did not *make* you.

"My new schedule means you may have to pack the kids' lunches on some mornings while I'm running around trying to get ready for dance," Mom told my father. He mumbled in return. A quiet strain remained apparent between them, but I thought it had more to do with the dust and the wind than with their natural dynamics. I'd seen the same strain, the same weariness, in the adults at school and in the grocery store whenever Mom took me shopping for new school supplies. Impatience. Irritation. A desire for the sky to go away and leave us alone.

Irritation shadowed the newspaper's front page. In the latest storm's wake, references to damage estimates, money amounts attached to repairs of houses and properties, dominated the first round of stories. But as the wind continued to whine, for days after the storm's onslaught, nerves frayed. The paper's reporting changed to reflect the community's need for emotional release. Dry financial estimates were replaced by profiles of children from well-to-do families suffering eye injuries or children hospitalized with respiratory infections when the dust clouds rolled into town. One reporter, exhibiting more resourcefulness than we were used to seeing from our local rag, convinced a physician from Midland Memorial Hospital to talk on record, listing the number of pediatric admissions he'd seen in the seven days after the storm: eighteen cases of silicosis, twenty-three instances of dust pneumonia, four young patients stricken with severe asthma (two of whom had collapsed on the San Jacinto practice football field), one case of hookworm. The numbers were astonishing—but it was that last word, "hookworm," almost a footnote to the story of the storm, that stuck in readers' minds. It has taken me many years to understand why this might have happened:

the storm coverage coincided with public disclosures—specific details—of the school board's Quonset hut deal.

Three classrooms, including one science lab, had been damaged at Carver High School by inclement weather, said the paper. The repair costs totaled $63,000. Local contractors estimated an eighteen-month repair window. An initiative instigated by Mr. Preston, but turned over to Mr. Seaker, allocated an unspecified amount of funding, approved by the school board, to upgrade one of the Quonset huts, purchase a limited amount of classroom furniture and supplies, and accommodate twelve Carver High seniors whose path toward timely graduation would otherwise be threatened by the loss of space at the high school. When the repairs to Carver's classrooms had been effected, the board would automatically revisit the Quonset huts' usefulness.

Critics of the plan, including some school board members, didn't hesitate to question Mr. Preston's altruism— though increasingly, attention fell on Mr. Seaker. It was all well and good to help disadvantaged students, these critics said, but the initiative's quiet implementation suggested a larger motive: a first step toward public school integration.

In the next two weeks, "hookworm" would become an effective weapon in public debates on the matter. I first heard a glimmer of this from my father, one morning at the breakfast table. He was lingering over the newspaper, avoiding making our lunches as our mother had asked him to do. She was back in her bedroom, pulling on her dance leotard. "Hookworm?" my father said. He rubbed his chin. "The storm didn't cause *that*. You get hookworm from parasites in the dirt—from walking around barefoot next to an outhouse." He said this was another old Okie disease he'd been quite familiar with growing up. The kids of poor farmers always had it. "Now, how did hookworm get into this part of town?"

I next heard this question in the grocery store, a few days later, when Mom dragged me on a shopping trip to choose the peanut butter I wanted ("I'm tired of hearing you complain about the 'tasteless' brand I buy"). Two women standing over tightly wrapped packages of frozen chicken thighs were speaking, in low voices, about "those peoples' kids" being "sneaked over" into "our" part of town. "Now, how does hookworm make its way into our neighborhoods?" one woman asked the other. "I think we know the answer." "Who came *up* with this idea? This cockamamie plan— why, those people don't want to be here anymore than we want them!" The first woman clucked her tongue. "It's that Seaker guy. Who *is* this guy, Seaker?"

"Flyboy and Slipjig!" Mary Louise's father called to them both and opened his arms to them beneath the green-and-white-striped awning above the brick patio. San Angelo had not suffered storms as intense as Midland's, but still, the town had been pelted with enough dust to make the cracks between the patio's bricks rough and gritty. The backyard, normally moist and green in late spring from

Mr. Thompson's watering and his careful cultivation, looked and smelled as dry as a winter desert.

Mr. Thompson—Bud was his name—pulled up two nylon chairs for his daughter and son-in-law. It was the occasion of their third wedding anniversary. They'd had a nice dinner out in a Midland restaurant, and an intimate evening together the night before, at the end of the school week. Now, here on the weekend, they had driven to San Angelo at Bud's invitation to celebrate with family. Mary Louise's mother and father would put them up for the night. Paul, Flyboy's younger brother, had finagled a forty-eight-hour pass from Webb, and he, too, would stay with the Thompsons, on a fold-out bed in the basement. He had not yet arrived from Big Spring.

As Flyboy and Slipjig settled into their patio chairs, Bud stirred a pitcher of ice cold margarita mix. "You want salt?" he asked, and they both said yes. Bud turned two large cocktail glasses upside down, ground their rims gently into a plate of Morton's, and then filled the glasses with the slushy green liquid. From inside the screen door into the kitchen, a perky dance rhythm rose and fell from an old phonograph: Mary Louise's favorite, "The Butterfly."

It was a pleasant early evening—winds calm, moderate temperature—and it would have been perfect were it not for the grit scratching under their feet and the occasional mosquito. Mary Louise's mother, Nan, brought two citronella candles from inside the house and set them on a patio table, a few feet from the chairs. She said she hoped the flames and the smell would draw the bugs away from their drinks.

Bud lighted an El Producto cigar, raised his glass and toasted the couple. He was a stocky man with heavy, whiskered jowls yellowed by tobacco. He resembled a bulldog, but not a *real* dog—more like a school's cartoon mascot. Next to him, Nan looked as thin as a chemistry beaker. "Three years now," she said. "Can your ol' ma expect grandkids anytime soon?"

"Mom!" Slipjig blushed, as red as the beets in the salad bowl. "Raymond's taking on more responsibilities each day at school. We're still a ways off from feeling settled enough to think about children."

Flyboy nodded. "Lately, I feel more like a nurse's aide than a vice principal. Quite a few of our kids have gotten sick as a result of these storms. I've made a handful of home visits, and even a couple of trips to the hospital."

Just the other night, he told his in-laws, he'd dropped by the Rodgers family's duplex after hearing about their daughter, Jessica, a third-grader—her right eyeball had suffered a scratch the day the third storm struck. The injury was severe enough to require a patch. Distraught, her mother had told the vice principal how worried she was that the trouble would restrict her daughter's progress in school. "She gets so fatigued, reading now with just the one eye. She can't keep up with her homework."

"Her teacher's aware of that, Mrs. Rodgers, and I assure you I'll keep reminding her to take good care of Jessica,"

Flyboy promised. "The persistence of these storms, this spring, has required us all to be flexible. We're working together to overcome the challenges."

"But why doesn't the school have a special room for this?"

"For what?"

"Storms! And my God, you should have a bomb shelter! I mean, you never really know!"

"No." Flyboy fell silent, and for the next half hour he let the woman exhaust her fears on him.

The following day, he had gone to see the Sheltons in their two-story ranch house in a just-completed subdivision north of town. Their boy, Charlie, had been diagnosed with pneumonia. "I didn't know you could catch a cold from too much dirt," the boy's father, a petroleum engineer, thick as an oak tree, said. His demure wife brought them coffee in the living room.

"Actually, I think it has more to do with the lungs . . . the respiratory passages," Flyboy started to say.

"You a doctor?" the man challenged him.

"No."

"Well, there you go."

Again, Flyboy remained quiet while a fearful parent ranted for half an hour about the uncertain times we lived in and the school's lack of preparation for handling emergencies. Nurse's aide? Maybe he was more like a priest— his main job was to listen.

His hardest visit had been to the hospital, just last week, where a fourth-grader named Frankie had been admitted with pneumonia, a critical case. Doctors had placed him on twenty-four-hour oxygen. His parents had been spending their nights in the waiting lounge, sleeping in thin plastic chairs. Flyboy offered them his fullest support, and said the school would do whatever it could to help Frankie readjust to the classroom when he felt well enough to return. "*If* he gets well enough to return," the boy's mother said. She was so limp with tears, such a wraith, she looked like a giant dishrag, twisted in a heap.

Her husband was the first parent Flyboy had met to raise—in addition to concerns about the school's poor storm preparations—the issue of the Quonset hut. "I seen in the paper that you got some . . . well, some kids from cross the tracks studyin' in one them old outbuildings."

"That's right," Flyboy answered carefully. He understood what a delicate subject it was, even among members of the school board. He didn't want to offer any more information than was necessary, not knowing where the man stood on the matter.

"I read how them kids had the dirt colds 'fore *our* kids ever got 'em."

"Well, I don't know," Flyboy answered. He wasn't sure where this was going, but it couldn't be anywhere good. Hastily, he repeated his condolences to the family, and hurried out of the hospital.

"So that's what the last few weeks have been like," he told his father-in-law now in the cool shadows of the backyard patio. Bud would understand his burdens, as a long-time school administrator. Flyboy welcomed his advice.

Bud flicked white ash from the tip of his cigar. "A lot of tough decisions fall to a man in a position of responsibility. I've read about your Quonset huts in the Midland paper. Tell me. What's this Mr. Preston up to? Is it purely a money-making deal for your school?"

"I think so, primarily—with the side benefits of really helping needy students, and of finding an excuse to fix up those old structures so they're not dangerous to the kids."

"The segregationists—the really immovable ones—they're mighty suspicious, I take it?"

"Naturally."

"Well, you're doing a good thing, Ray. But slow and careful—that's your method. I figure change'll happen more or less quickly in the cities, Dallas and Houston and the like. But the schools in West Texas—they'll never be fully integrated until the courts get more involved."

"I hear you."

"Oh, enough gloomy old politics!" Slipjig interjected. "The Dunmore Lasses" was playing on the phonograph now. She rose, held out her hand, and pulled Flyboy out of his chair. She danced him around the patio until they'd doubled over laughing.

The evening only got better with Paul's arrival. He was dreamily handsome in his military uniform, Slipjig declared. Slender and strapping. Like his older brother, he had sharp, avian features, but his hair and skin were darker, and his cheeks were mottled, the after-effect of adolescent acne, all of which invested him with a rough-hewn quality.

From Bud, he gladly accepted a salty margarita, and caught the others up on his latest training drills at Webb. From his status as student, just a short time ago, he had graduated to serving as an instructor pilot with the Lockheed T-33 "Shooting Stars," a variant of the old P-80 jet fighters Flyboy had cut his teeth on years ago.

"Every day, I'm up there high above the clouds with these young recruits," Paul said proudly.

Bud asked, "Is the base on—I don't know what the term would be, 'High Alert?'—since stories broke about that Russian nuclear incident?"

Paul said, "I can't talk about the 'Soviet matter,' but as long as Korea stays hot, we've got to keep up with our drills."

"Amen to that," Bud answered.

Paul toasted the "newlyweds."

"Nah, we're an old married couple now," Flyboy said, and laughed.

"Three years? Still counts as fresh, in my book."

Bud went into the kitchen to stir up another pitcher of drinks. Nan accepted Slipjig's offer to shuck the corncobs and slice the potatoes for supper. Flyboy stood with Paul in the dusty yard, reminiscing about their family. Their grandfather had never expected them to become cotton farmers, as he had been; they would enjoy the advantage of college, and of greater financial opportunities—it was a generational thing, and precisely the way a family's evolution should run. But the old man insisted they never shirk physical activity, no matter how studious or desk-bound they became. From earliest youth, they learned from him the rigors of daily exercise: hauling bales of cotton from the sunny fields to the beds of the trucks, lifting crates of tools using the muscles in their legs.

After a long day, during harvest season, the brothers would sit together in their grandmother's kitchen, gulping her lemonade, listening to her program on the radio—inspirational stories from "people just like you." If Paul or Flyboy complained of a sore back, their grandpop would chide them for lousy work habits. "You're not using your thighs as a fulcrum, centering your gravity there, like I taught you," he'd say. "You're going to grow up like a pair of old washer women, curled over a steel tub!"

In his father-in-law's modest yard, Flyboy laughed now, slapping Paul's shoulder. "And now, most of those old cotton fields have been annexed into the airfield. Incredible."

"The equipment's getting better, Ray. Every day. You wouldn't believe it. Our techniques are getting sharper. I'm going to be twice the pilot you were!"

Flyboy didn't doubt it. He raised his margarita glass in a swift, crisp salute, and then he drained what was left of his drink. He couldn't have been prouder of his little brother.

Four days after the word "hookworm" first appeared in the *Midland Reporter-Telegram*, the top fold of the paper's front page was devoted to a picture of a suffering kid from our school. The child was not afflicted with hookworm, but was nevertheless presented as a warning to *Reporter-Telegram* readers: "Accidentally, walls of a safe quarantine may have been toppled," the caption claimed. It is clear in retrospect (as it was not clear at the time) that certain members of the school board, opponents of *Brown v. Board of Education*, had ties to the newspaper's managing editor, and were able to insert their opinions as facts into the mainstream news.

It is clear that Mr. Preston, whatever he was trying to accomplish, had anticipated this development and had established a screen between him and public backlash. "According to sources at Midland Memorial Hospital"— sources never identified—"Vice Principal Raymond Seaker's 'experiment' of providing classroom space to Negro students may well result in viral epidemics in heretofore healthy areas of town, the likes of which our city has never experienced."

In addition to its front page "investigation," editorials on the paper's opinion page called on Raymond Seaker to defend the rationale behind his decision to admit "infectious agents" into public schools west of Midland's Southern Pacific Railroad tracks.

The front page photograph was a candid shot taken from the rear. Because its subject's face was obscured, therefore not immediately identifiable, and because other persons (also ambiguous) appeared in the field, permission from the subject or the subject's family was not required for the paper to publish the image.

The "afflicted child," the harbinger of doom from the other side of the tracks, was a frail-limbed boy hobbling on crutches near the Quonset huts on the playground's southern edge.

# 6.

Stevie, of course, had nothing to do with hookworm or the Quonset hut "experiment," but he became the image of panic. As a result of his notoriety, taunts of "Gimp" gave way to "Worm! Worm! Gasper and the Worm!"

Really, the other kids didn't ostracize him much more than they had in the past, though parents visibly flinched if they happened to glimpse him while picking up their children after school. At recess, he and I retreated farther from our healthy classmates. We avoided the huts. We became aware of newspaper photographers lurking at the edges of the playground: pasty-faced men in hot suits lugging tripods and other awkward equipment. We pointed them out to Mr. Seaker. On two or three occasions, he marched across the field to confront them. "These are children!" he shouted. "Leave them alone." It was not lost on us that these incidents were parodies of his standoff with the "Messkins," the moment that, only a short time earlier, had made him a hero. His mornings were no longer feasts prepared by grateful mothers. One day, a woman emerged from her car as it sat idling at a crosswalk and yelled at him, across the dusty field, "Flyboy, get rid of those nasty kids from 'cross the tracks!"

One morning, during early recess, seven or eight girls

in brown plaid dresses carried their skip ropes onto the field. Singing 'You Can Fly,' they took turns jumping in and out of swirling loops. They got a little too close to the huts. Apparently, the plumbing had failed that day. One of the Carver High students had stepped out back to relieve himself.

Screams. Nervous laughter.

The girls sprinted to Mr. Seaker's office, swinging their ropes like whips. Dee Dee was part of the pack. "His *thing*! It was just out there in the open, waving, like *this*!" she told Mr. Seaker. Naturally, despite his admonishments to the group to remain quiet about this until he had time to investigate the situation, they went home and told their moms.

Since taking up dance, our mother seemed to me significantly more hobbled than before. She was always complaining of a sore back, sore thighs. She had blisters on her feet. She insisted she was stronger, more limber, a whirlwind of energy. She had seized control of her life and would no longer allow herself to be sidelined. But whereas she had not seemed particularly stressed to me in the past, she now overreacted to the slightest provocation. "Oh my God!" she cried when Dee Dee told her what had happened. She didn't bother to ferret out details. Other mothers responded much the same, so of course it was not possible to keep the story from the paper.

By the time the news appeared in the *Reporter-Telegram*, it had become a case of "Negro boy exposes himself to young girls." The story appeared on the front page next to an article proclaiming the "Quonset hut experiment" phase one in an attempt to integrate the city's sports teams. In the next few days, this rumor unraveled. Apparently, a reporter had misheard the San Jacinto football coach, who'd remarked in passing that the recent dust storms had wreaked such havoc with his team's practices, "it might be a blessing to have some of them kids from 'cross town fill in for us at certain key positions. After all, they're state champs ever' year."

Even with *that* story's retraction, the hue and cry in our community had reached such fever pitch, the school board called an emergency meeting. During this period, Mr. Preston seemed conspicuously missing from school. Whether he was, I'm not certain. I never kept track of him anyway, so it may be I'm simply misremembering. In any case, Mr. Seaker was the school's public face throughout the crisis.

The downtown firehouse, where the school board gathered for its meetings, was equipped with a series of small conference rooms on its second floor. The first floor was devoted to Midland's conflagrations: framed black-and-white photographs of the great infernos of the past. Wilson's Feed Store, reduced to cinders, 1898. The First Baptist Church, badly charred, 1907. Sadie's Dog Grooming Parlor, an unspeakable tragedy, 1923. The hose and ax of Midland's first fire chief, Otis MacKennon, were enshrined behind glass, next to the staircase to the second floor. One hot night in late May, grim parents paid homage to the chief's sacred tools as they tramped up the steps to the central conference room. As one parent put it, they had come to hear Mr. Seaker address "what in the heck they was thinkin' when they opened the floodgates, lettin' just *anyone* into our schools."

"Integration is a complicated process, full of legal and logistical complexities. The Midland Independent School District has not yet approached it in any formal capacity," Mr. Seaker told the crowd, so large it was standing room only. Lines wound around the small space, out the door, back down the stairs. School board members scowled behind Mr. Seaker as he stood gripping the podium's edges. "I assure you, the Quonset hut classroom is a temporary measure, designed to relieve Carver High School of its space pressures as a result of storm damage."

"Why not move the students to another Negro school, in *their* part of town?" someone asked.

"None of the facilities in those areas are adequate."

"What are *we* getting out of the deal?"

"We're not losing any funding, if that's what you're worried about," Mr. Seaker said. "We're being compensated by the district, so we can continue to—"

"Are we making a profit?"

"That's not the way to look at this, if I may. Our mission is to educate the children of this town. *All* the children. We believe we've found a creative solution to a singular challenge. We're happy to help—in fact, we're *duty-bound* to help our colleagues and the children of our neighbors."

"Whose neighbors? They're not *our* neighbors."

"But they are," Mr. Seaker said.

A groan rose from the crowd.

"Those twelve students from Carver High School—they're now going to have an opportunity to graduate. They'll have a leg up on the future, and who knows what the future will hold for them? They may make Midland proud someday."

Shouting, talking, whispering in the audience.

"By *exposing* themselves to our kids?"

"No, no, that—"

"And spreading God knows what diseases?"

"I don't think Flyboy did himself, or your school, any favors last night," Dad said the following morning, skimming the paper. He poured himself some coffee. "The more he tried to squelch the rumors, the louder they became."

"He says it's always good to talk things out," I said. "He says, 'Dialogue is the key to progress.'"

"I don't know," Dad said. "This town's like a powder keg, ready to blow."

And then it did.

At 1:51 p.m. on May 22, 1957, a Cessna 107A, a single-engine prop plane, left the Midland County Airport bound for Ruidoso, New Mexico. Five souls filled its seats, members of a prominent local family on their way to a vacation retreat: the pilot, his wife, their infant daughter, and the wife's parents. The plane banked northward just off the runway, and then it made a southwest turn. At this same moment,

the fourth major dust storm of the season was brewing—
with unexpected swiftness—thirty miles east of Midland
and heading straight for the heart of the basin. At 1:59,
convection currents had become so powerful at ground
level, all further flights out of Midland County Airport were
canceled. But the Cessna was already in the air.

At 1:23 p.m., a Lockheed T-33 "Shooting Star" had de-
parted Webb Air Force Base in Big Spring on a training
mission. Its task was to perform ILS (Instrument Land-
ing System) approaches at the Midland Airport. The purpose of the ILS drills was to teach young pilots to land
in restricted-visibility conditions. Darkness. Fog. Dust.
The drill called for the student pilot, strapped into the aft
seat, to wear a hood attachment on his helmet, blacking
out everything but his cockpit instruments and simulat-
ing real-world experience. The instructor pilot, occupy-
ing the jet's forward seat, remained alert for hazards or
other aircraft. The jet maintained constant contact with
the Midland tower. It had already performed a successful
touch-and-go on the north runway, and had been granted
permission for a second approach when, at 1:52, Midland
lost the T-33. A wave of dust rolled over town. The boiling
brown clouds crackled with electricity. Immediately, vis-
ibility dropped to zero. The dust swelled as high as thir-
ty-one thousand feet. Shortly after two o'clock, dozens of
Midland residents phoned the police emergency line to report red flames and plumes of black smoke shooting high
into the haze.

The T-33 had struck the Cessna from behind at a sharply descending angle, slicing apart its left side, its rudder ripping through the Cessna's thin aluminum structure. The jet's tail separated from the body of the plane. The civilian craft broke into five major pieces. The instructor pilot ejected from the T-33, but he didn't have sufficient altitude for his parachute to open before he slammed into the front lawn of a new house in a northern subdivision just off Interstate 80, causing the automatic sprinkler system to activate and turn the blowing dust into a wall of vibrating mud. Later, the instructor's corpse was found buried in muck three inches thick. The student pilot, trapped in his seat, trying frantically to wriggle loose by disconnecting his oxygen hose, hurtled in a flaming chunk of wreckage straight into the sand trap of a local golf course, kicking up another little storm.

The family in the Cessna was thrown in wildly different directions. The plane's engine crashed through the roof of an auto supply store just west of downtown Midland. Thirty seconds later, the pilot came shooting through the hole in the roof. He landed right where the engine had, in a scattered pool of fan belts and shattered cans of 10W-40. None of the store's employees were injured.

The infant's body landed in the flower bed of a modest home near San Jacinto Junior High, the bluebonnets printed on its cotton PJs matching those in the garden where the baby came to rest. The pilot's wife and her parents fell onto houses west of our school, plunging through hot, cluttered attics. The wife wound up in a bathtub.

Over two hours passed before the bodies could be removed, and all the wreckage located, because the dust was so thick on the streets, emergency vehicles could not maneuver.

Later, investigators attributed the accident to instructor error. The T-33 trainer couldn't see the Cessna in the sudden gusts of dust. Having lost radio contact with the Midland tower, he received no warnings.

At the time of the mid-air calamity, my mother had taken to her bed again with another migraine, depressed that her dance routines had not cured her of her malady. She lay in the yellow dark, curtains loosely closed, moaning slightly. I had left school early, with my teacher's permission. My father had picked me up and dropped me off at home before returning to work, so I could breathe the moist air of the humidifier. In the midst of our town's hysteria over the spread of disease, my mother and I stayed still and silent together, tending our ailments. We didn't know until the following day about the air disaster.

"I *thought* I heard a loud boom early in the afternoon," Mom said, "but I chalked it up to thunder or the throbbing in my head." We learned from the television that the T-33 instructor pilot's name was Paul Seaker.

I'm certain that the following days' events could only have occurred in that place, at that time, in a manner that might not have been inevitable were it not for storm-fatigue, the awful irritation of the dust, the screaming of the wind. By that point, too, the name "Seaker" had appeared often in the newspaper, attached to unpleasant developments in the schools—even the hastiest readers knew that by now. The name produced an almost Pavlovian effect.

And the backdrop: the community's fears of radiation, nuclear war (exacerbated by a plane crash over town). The unleashing of disease. The blurring of our once well-established neighborhoods, so a fellow didn't exactly know where he stood in Midland anymore.

Then, the shared public grief. The Cessna family had been well-loved by Midland's prominent citizens, including the mayor, the newspaper's managing editor, and some powerful friends of the family serving on the school board. Who had killed them all? A man named Seaker.

Someone may have said it first as a morbid joke—one of those dark remarks intended to see us through hard times. Something like, "Those Seaker boys—they're out to get us all!" Something like, "First it's our schools, then it's our skies. What's next?" An offhand comment at the end of a school board meeting. Or on the ninth fairway at the country club's golf course. Or in a restaurant, over dessert wine. The Seaker Plan. The Seaker Plot. Then the Seaker Conspiracy.

At school, we heard that Mr. Seaker was going to take a week off, to arrange and attend his brother's funeral. His prolonged absence left Stevie and me exposed and vulnerable on the playground. We were standing near the jungle gym one day. Stevie was telling me how he'd like to be a scientist—a physicist, maybe, or an astronomer. Maybe he'd study the dust storms on Mars.

"Gasper! Worm!" someone called. A clutch of our classmates approached—four tall boys. It was the end of afternoon recess. They surrounded us. "So. Ain't got your commie buddy to look after you today!" said the leader.

"Mr. Seaker's not a commie," I snapped. I puffed my chest.

"Sure he is." Like the others, this boy had adored Mr. Seaker until the Quonset huts made the news, and his parents started talking. "My mama says commies're wrecking our schools, lettin' in those peoples' kids."

"Your mama doesn't know what she's saying," I said.

"You don't talk about my mama!" The boy shoved me to the ground—a hard jab to the stomach. I lay in the dirt, trying to breathe. "And you." He turned to Stevie. "Don't you come around here spreadin' hookworm." He grabbed Stevie's crutches and hurled them across the field in the direction of the Quonset huts. "Got it, Worm?"

Stevie couldn't walk at all without his crutches. We'd be late now, returning to class. The boys laughed and ran toward the classroom buildings.

"Give me a minute," I told Stevie. I pulled my inhaler from my back pocket. "I'll go get them."

As I struggled to stand, I glanced up. Against the beige sky, its dark brown streaks, I saw a black boy emerge from the middle hut, wearing jeans and a red Carver High

T-shirt. He was tall and skinny, with gangly arms sway-ing gracefully like the limbs of a willow. He made for Ste-vie's crutches, picked them up, and brought them to us. He smelled like sweat and freshly mown grass. Wide-eyed, Stevie stared at the boy's angular face. "Thank you," he said quietly.

"I was watching," the boy said.

I got to my feet. I felt the gravity of the moment—and it wasn't just the weight in my chest. "It's brave of you to come outside like this," I said.

He shrugged, his bony shoulders like knife blades poking up through his thin cotton shirt. "No problem. Don't like to see big kids picking on littler ones. Used to happen to me all the time."

"Thanks."

"Sure," he said.

"What's your name?"

He smiled at me. He said nothing. He turned and walked back to the hut.

Simple. Swift. Just like that, Stevie and I had crossed a line. We had *integrated*. He adjusted his crutches un-der his armpits. We were late for class but neither of us moved. We stood there, stunned and all by ourselves on the playground.

# 7.

"He was the *real* Flyboy," Flyboy said. "May God grant you wings, little brother."

He was standing over Paul's lacquered casket in the Big Spring funeral parlor. Slipjig held his hand. The room was stuffy and hot. Red wax paper had been taped to the windows to dim the light. The colored squares reminded him of a bad craft project undertaken by first-graders.

His dress loafers were scuffed from the grit on the parlor's oak floor. He had polished the shoes just that morning. Somehow, Slipjig had managed to maintain her freshness in the heat. Her hair remained neatly pinned in the back. Though she was sweating, her crinoline dress stayed crisp and cool to the touch.

That's because she still has a future, Flyboy thought, shocked by his blunt despair. But it was true. Until he'd heard the story of Paul's death, he'd measured his enthusiasm for the future by the plans he shared with Slipjig, by his career progress. Vice principal; maybe, in five years, moving up to principal and then to a position of responsibility with the school district. A modest, one-bedroom starter house; a child (boy); a second child (girl); a larger home in one of the new subdivisions north of town . . . it was easy to envision, and not at all impossible to realize.

But now it was gone for him.

Without Paul in the picture, the talented younger brother to advance the family's long investment in flight, relieving Flyboy of that awesome necessity, the future meant nothing. Worse: it didn't exist.

Flyboy had loved to soar. The high, golden clouds breaking like foam against his cockpit window always thrilled him. But when, in his hard bunk at Goodfellow Field, he had awakened in the dark to the nightmarish screams of men suffering "fatigue," men who'd leapt from burning planes to save themselves, he'd reconfigured the future. Slipjig had been the leap he'd made, and it *had* saved his meager life— Slipjig and her admiration for his ease with children, a skill he'd never known he'd possessed. He'd embraced these new possibilities with immense gratitude. But not until this moment, reeling above his brother's casket, had he recognized how completely his choices had depended on Paul fulfilling the family's devotion to the sky. And he'd done so brilliantly, with energy and expansive gifts for navigation.

But *this*, now: his extinguishment, and in a manner paralleling the nightmares of those poor wretches in the barracks . . . exposing, in retrospect, Flyboy's behavior: his cowardice, refusing to fly anymore. Nothing, no one, had been saved, after all.

The day was sunny and mild, but the air remained turgid with dust particles. Mercifully, the minister kept the graveside service short. Flyboy had to physically fight the urge to jump into the hole in the ground after his brother's coffin, as the mourners turned, silent, to leave the cemetery.

That night, back in his house in Midland, Flyboy went to bed early, right after supper. "Exhausted," he mumbled. Slipjig wriggled free of her nightgown. She slid in beside him under the sheet. It was not like her to initiate love-making, but she moved on top of him and kissed his lips urgently, as if she recognized how thoroughly he'd relinquished any claim to the days ahead. "Let's make a baby," she whispered, and all he could picture was flaming metal casings hurtling to earth.

He rebuffed her as gently as he could, but she wept as he turned over, away from her, and he lay awake most of the night, mourning, feeling guilty about his wife, aware that she was awake, too, still and quiet, waiting for the smallest signal from him. He remembered Paul as a boy, on the roof of their grandfather's barn, cradling a black-and-white kitten to his chest. Paul had fashioned wings from the pages of a newspaper, and fastened them with rubber bands to the kitten's trembling legs. The kitten yowled. Paul called down to Flyboy, standing next to a truck bed filled with cotton. "Grandpa says cats always land on their feet. Maybe they can learn to fly." And he tossed the kitten from the roof. He missed the truck bed. The poor thing *did* land on its feet, hard, on the ground, but when Paul scrambled down the loft ladder and saw the limping animal, he became inconsolable. He grabbed his brother's shirt and cried against his shoulders. "What did I do? What did I do?"

"Some things weren't made for the air," Flyboy remembered telling his brother that day.

Now he wiped the tears from his eyes. Next to him, Slipjig sniffled. He turned and stroked her shoulder. "I'm sorry," he whispered, "I'm sorry," and he pulled her into his arms.

His first two days back at school were uneventful. The kids were quiet and respectful. On the third morning, Mr. Preston called him into his office.

Flyboy had a hard time figuring Preston out. The man was kind to him, invariably polite, but remote. He always made very clear what he wanted Flyboy to do, but he'd never share the larger vision, the goals, the outcomes of his initiatives. Like this Quonset hut business. The message seemed to be: *you* implement my plans so I can grow my résumé and get out of here. Flyboy was happy to go along if it meant they all moved up the administrative ladder.

He hadn't seen Preston in a couple of weeks. Of course, he'd been busy with his brother's funeral. A bank of windows in Preston's office overlooked the playground. Preston sat at his desk like a monarch surveying his empire. Framed pictures crowded the desktop: Preston's wife, Catherine, hugging her toy poodle, Max. The dog was wide and flat-looking. It reminded Flyboy of a tropical fish. He'd only met Catherine twice, at school board socials. She struck him as a woman determined not to spend the rest of her life in the West Texas desert.

"I suppose you've seen this?" Preston said to Flyboy, motioning him into a chair and offering him the front page of the *Midland Reporter-Telegram*. Flyboy hadn't had time to glance at the paper this morning. Now, he stared at his face, his younger face as it had appeared in the *Lampasas Dispatch* on April 2, 1952. He was wearing a blocky military uniform with epaulets. Beneath his grainy image, a caption said, "We are at war with the United States army and its generals, who are nothing more than political gangsters." The *Reporter-Telegram* called for an immediate investigation into Raymond Seaker's "war-time activities." The article did not mention communism but the insinuation was clear.

Flyboy laughed. "This is ridiculous."

"The dozens of school parents who've phoned me so far this morning don't seem to think so," Preston said. He was a small man who—despite his aggressive manner—gave an overall impression of continuous withdrawal.

"That picture . . . it was part of a military exercise. Operation Longhorn," Flyboy said. "We pretended to take over a town so the boys could get training in urban fighting and counterinsurgency. I posed as an invading propaganda minister. The Lampasas paper printed this as a special edition . . . it's fake! Clearly."

"Well. I'm afraid that's not so clear to our parents."

"I can't believe . . . I mean, come on! The *Reporter-Tele-*

*gram* knows this is fake! If they've got hold of the paper, they know it says, 'FOR MANUEVER PURPOSES ONLY,' right below the masthead."

"There's no mention of that."

"Then it's character assassination, pure and simple. Someone's out to get me. *Us.* The school." He slumped in his chair. "It's because they don't want those Carver kids here."

Preston nodded. "Yes. I suspect that's right. And I believe you, Ray, but—"

"Look, it's easy to debunk. Call Goodfellow. Call Webb. Call the former mayor of Lampasas. They'll all tell you—"

"In the meantime, *this* is the story that's out there, and we have to deal with the fallout."

"Are you firing me?"

"No, Ray. But we're going to have to come up with a plan of action."

As it turned out, the story was not as easy to discredit as Flyboy thought it would be. The official spokespeople at Goodfellow and Webb Air Force Base were reluctant to confirm the existence of Operation Longhorn in the tense Cold War atmosphere, especially following rumors of a recent nuclear accident in the Soviet Union. The archives of the *Lampasas Dispatch* no longer kept copies of the special edition. Apparently, the *Reporter-Telegram* had obtained the paper from the son of a Lampasas resident at the time of the exercise. Whether the son or the reporter from the Midland paper knew what they were looking at or whether the article was a deliberate smear wasn't clear.

Three days later, the paper printed a small retraction on page nine, admitting that the photograph and the treasonous words had apparently been part of a war game some years ago. But the damage had been done. More people had seen the picture than would read the correction. And by then, the school board had scheduled a meeting at the firehouse to discuss the future of Raymond Seaker's Quonset hut initiative.

Once again, a crowd filled the room to capacity, blocked the hallway, and snaked down the stairs past the old fire chief's wooden ax. The audience remained awkwardly silent as school board members asked Mr. Seaker to provide them with a progress report on the "Carver arrangement." He said he was happy to inform the board that the upgraded facility had served its purpose quite splendidly, that the teachers had indicated the supplies were more than adequate, and that the students were having a productive and favorable experience. "And what would you say the major gains from this experiment have been?" asked the board's chair.

"A dozen Carver High students who would probably not have graduated on time are now on track to receive their diplomas at the end of this school year," Flyboy answered.

"*They* graduate. And *our* kids get sick!" someone shouted from the back of the room. Several people cheered.

Mr. Seaker raised his hand. "There is no indication that any of the relocated students have introduced illnesses into our community."

"Hookworm! It's rampant!"

"*One* reported case," Flyboy reminded everyone.

"It didn't come from *our* neighborhoods."

"Apparently it did." This remark set off a round of jeers. The board never regained control of the meeting. Before the chair pounded his gavel to adjourn, multiple accusations of "foreign interference in our school system" and "plans to undermine American education" had been hurled at the vice principal, who seemed to visibly diminish behind the podium.

That night in bed, Flyboy hugged his wife and said he wasn't sure he recognized his town anymore. "My God, you should have seen their faces. The fear. The anger. No. It was hatred. How did everything get so confused?"

"I don't know, sweetie."

"War. Sickness. Black kids, white kids . . . these things have nothing to *do* with one another, and yet . . ."

Slipjig kissed his mouth. "Let's make a baby," she said.

He'd had enough of goddamn Martian dust storms. The boys were sweet, well-meaning, and curious. But their discussions of the Red Planet on the playground, every day without variation, had grown tedious. It was amazing how kids could seize on something, a word, an idea, like pit bulls pouncing on prey.

Exactly the way grief had seized on him. Grief—and

more than grief. An abdication of the body's demand, the mind's hope that he *go on*.

What for? he thought. Go on for what?

The school was a prison now and he was being punished. Punished for refusing to fly. Punished for the death of his brother. He'd lost his touch with kids. How could he ever be a father?

He stood in the middle of the field, waiting for the children to burst from their classrooms, a cyclone of shouting, laughing, mismatched colors whirling toward the monkey bars. He stared at the Quonset huts. Empty today, bland and hollow. Mr. Preston had ordered him to suspend the Carver High lessons until Preston decided how to address the fury of the school board meeting.

Polar caps. Maybe, at least, I could get them to talk about Martian ice sheets instead, Flyboy thought. A sudden, planet-wide freeze.

The bell rang. Doors banged open. As he turned to face the onslaught, a Ford station wagon came to a stop at the crosswalk on the wide avenue east of the playground. The driver's side door sprang open. A woman in a purple muumuu, her black hair wrapped in curlers, stepped out of the car and yelled at him, "Commie!"

# 8.

My father sang loudly in the Oldsmobile about a dust storm sweeping away his home. His pecan tree had finally succumbed to the winds. We'd gotten up on a Saturday morning to find its slender black trunk bowed all the way to the ground, roots exposed, limbs snapped. My father set his mouth grimly, his face tight and pale. He didn't say a word until half an hour after breakfast, when he asked, "Want to make a well run with me?"

I understood we were making this trip in lieu of sitting in the yard feeling helpless. I understood from him it was always good to have work to turn to.

He drove us out to an old discovery well, a wooden rig sitting long defunct in the desert at the eastern edge of Midland County. This relic didn't need inspecting. He was feeling wistful. He had an urge to ruminate. "I was a wildcatter on this operation," he told me. "We spudded her out ten years ago. She began producing right away. The drill encountered a show of oil at about 450 feet, but I talked my boss at the time into going even deeper, and at 2,100 feet we had us a *well*. A real beauty of a pay horizon. For the next five years, it was one hundred barrels a day. Modest but steady. We finally had to water-flood her a couple of years ago, but she helped put our company on the map."

He turned in a slow circle, taking in every quadrant of the hazy beige horizon. "Every town in this basin, every family, is here because some old rockhound poked a hole in the earth." With the back of his hand he wiped the sweat from his face. "And now I guess the earth has whipped up these winds to take it all back. Someday there won't be a trace of anything we've done here, good or bad. Well. Who knows? Given what's happened lately, maybe that's a blessing."

We returned in silence to the car. I didn't quite grasp his mood but I knew he didn't want to talk. He placed his hand on my shoulder. As we passed the rig, in the shadows of its girders, he stepped on a loose wooden plank in the dirt. A rusty nail jutted crookedly out of the plank; it entered the tender meat of my father's right foot, straight through the sole of his shoe. He fell to the ground, groaning. "Troy! Troy, you're going to have to pull it out!" I shook my head. "Listen to me, son, grab hold of that thing, one hand on either side . . . yes, just like that . . . now *yank*!" I fell backwards on my butt, gripping the plank, the exposed nail bubbling with my father's blood.

Gingerly, moaning like my mother with a headache, he slipped off his shoe and his sock. His foot was as white as the marbled fat on a slice of bacon. It trembled, and the blood smelled sweet. He tied his sock around his instep, a loose tourniquet. "Pull me up now," he said through gritted teeth. When he'd got upright, he leaned on my shoulder and we hobbled to the car.

On the way to the emergency room, I squeezed his right thigh with both hands, hard, to keep him from passing out whenever he pressed his injured foot to the brake. It seemed little enough to do but later he said my steady pressure on his leg had been essential, helping him focus, and he credited me with getting us to the hospital.

He endured a tetanus shot; afterward, he enjoyed a swift recovery, and the incident would hardly be worth mentioning if not for its meaning for me later—the twin realizations that my father was capable of being diminished by circumstance (and he knew it—that's why he'd made that wistful trip to the rig that day, to face the truth of it) and I was capable of trading places with him. In fact, I'd be *required* to take his place in time, as I grew strong and he grew weaker with age.

I imagine that day he felt something akin to Mr. Seaker's experience (as reported to me later): confusion about the recent events in his town, in his life, which is to say *bafflement with change, and an inability to stop it*. For my father, the confusion appeared to begin the morning he lost his pecan tree. For the longest time, I figured him this way: he had planted a seed in the desert, his personal stake in the place, hoping, against towering odds, it would flourish. It didn't. The dust came, the wind came, and he'd had to accept that he had little control over the pace of his days.

And this was true enough, as far as it went. Now, of course, with the benefit of time, with the wider angle it provides, I see what else eluded my father's control: my mother's headaches, her growing irritation with his coddling of her, his town's changing demographics, its divisive politics, and the consequences of these developments for his children's futures.

Just an old rockhound, spudding out wherever he could, until the dusty old dust blew in and swept everything away.

The tree was the least of it, that morning.

Just as Mars was the least of it the day Mr. Seaker told me abruptly on the playground he didn't have time for me.

In that season of dust, in the spring of 1957, the elements that formed my innocence (and perhaps that of my father and Mr. Seaker, as well)—family, school, health, earth and sky—were in place, but no more firmly planted than my father's gesture, with the tree, to make a stake, to say *This is who I am and this is where I belong*, not knowing that neither half of that statement could ever be constant.

# 9.

Slipjig and Flyboy never made a baby. They divorced in 1962, following Flyboy's third dismissal as a substitute teacher in a rural Texas town, after he'd resigned from the Midland Independent School District in 1958. When he'd decided he didn't have a future, the day he'd buried his brother Paul, he'd meant it, he told Stevie Williston, when he and Stevie got reacquainted in Big Spring in the early 1980s.

Stevie had abandoned his dream of becoming a scientist—"I wasn't good enough at math," he told me initially. He'd settled, instead, for being a real estate developer after completing a couple of correspondence courses in the field. It was a good time to broker deals in West Texas, he said: oil was up over forty dollars a barrel, and hangars were sitting empty out at the old Webb Air Force Base. In the space of four years, from 1968 to 1972, Stevie developed on the base's old site (on parcels of land once owned by the Seaker family) a drag racing track, a Fina refinery complex, a Coca-Cola bottling plant, a limestone block processor, and a private school for the hearing impaired. He had become a wealthy man, happily married, unexpected outcomes for someone who'd just stumbled into his career.

"Really, the math had nothing to do with it," he confessed

eventually when I met him for lunch one day at the Petroleum Club in downtown Midland ("Pretty fancy digs," Stevie said, looking around at the plush chairs and the glass chandeliers). This was 1983. We were balding, middle-aged men. I had become a geologist, as my father had been. "I didn't pursue science because I didn't have the confidence for it, or for much of anything else." He pointed to his crutches—aluminum now, sleek, flexible, not the stiff wooden sticks he'd wielded as a child. "I never got past being the 'Gimp.' I'm ashamed to say I let it hold me back."

I told him I was impressed by how self-aware he was, and how honest he could be about himself.

"Well. It helps that I've been so successful in spite of my hang-ups. You? Your asthma?"

"I seem to have outgrown it."

"Lucky."

"Yes. And so . . . Mr. Seaker? You just bumped into him?" I asked.

Stevie nodded. "He told me he'd moved back to Big Spring several years ago. Of course, he didn't recognize me—he remembered me as a kid—but I knew him right away. Though he's in pretty bad shape. Seems he had a bout of TB some time back—he blames it on dust. Lost a lot of weight. A real scarecrow. He just seems to me . . . I don't know, he seems like a fellow who gave up." Stevie said the former vice principal was working now for a developer of private prisons in West Texas, southern Oklahoma, and eastern New Mexico.

"If you come to Big Spring some time, I could introduce you to him."

"No," I said. "I don't think I could bear to see him the way you describe him."

He told Stevie the details of his life—the ones I've related here (along with some small speculation on my part). Shortly after the appearance of Mr. Seaker's picture in the *Midland Reporter-Telegram* that spring, after the accusations of Mr. Seaker being a communist traitor, Mr. Preston decided to end the Carver High "experiment." He ordered Mr. Seaker to announce that the twelve black students would no longer be accommodated at our school, citing financial considerations, and to say that a planning group would be convened to determine future uses of the huts. Five years later, after sitting empty again, they were demolished.

"None of the Carver High students graduated on time, and seven of them never graduated at all," Flyboy told Stevie the third or fourth time they'd met for drinks. "When I heard that—well, that's when I resigned my position as vice principal and decided to leave Midland." He could not forgive himself for bowing to pressure and letting down those kids, he said. "They were innocents—just being used, tossed back and forth in the town's guilty spasms."

"But you can't blame yourself," Stevie argued with him. "You were ordered to do it—*all* of it—by your boss."

"Who moved to California. I suppose you heard?"

"No."

"Yeah. Took a job with the State Education Department there. Hailed as a forward-thinker. An early champion of integration. Anyway, Slipjig said what you said—that I shouldn't blame myself."

"And?"

He shook his head. "I could've taken a stand. Against Preston. The school board. All those angry, ignorant people in town."

"The result would've been the same," Stevie assured him. "The students would still have been banished across the tracks. And you'd have been fired."

"But I wouldn't have been a coward. The way I was at Goodfellow, spooked by all those guys afraid to fly. So what did I do? I quit the Air Force."

"And got married. To a wonderful girl. And got a wonderful job. A *rational* decision, I'd say."

Flyboy wriggled his shoulders—a slump more than a shrug.

"Did you tell your wife you considered yourself a coward? At Goodfellow?" Stevie asked.

"Eventually . . . she knew how I felt."

"I suppose that didn't help the marriage?"

"No."

"And where is she now?"

"Houston. Remarried. Two kids. Happy, as far as I know. I think of her now and then, especially whenever I hear an old reel, you know, but . . ."

Stevie reported to me that, in their get-togethers, Mr.

Seaker spoke to him neither passionately nor indifferently, neither enthusiastically nor reluctantly. He was penitential, perhaps, confessing without emotion only because Stevie asked him the questions, and only because Stevie, as one of the kids in his charge that spring, *deserved* the answers. He was forthcoming in a teacherly way—as if he was proud of Stevie for maturing and being capable of intelligent interrogation.

"Above all, he gave off an air of failure," Stevie told me. "Not just physical decline from the TB and years of obvious self-neglect, lack of good nutrition—but utter demoralization. I was looking at who *I* would have been had I not gotten lucky, I thought. My bad hip had accustomed me to living with low self-esteem, you know, to thinking of myself as unattractive, incapable of excellence. I was used to being mocked, overlooked, dismissed. But Mr. Seaker! The military vet! The man who'd vanquished the Messkins!"

I laughed.

"How could *he* have been stopped so easily? While I . . . I turned everything around. Admittedly with good fortune, and without really knowing I was doing it. Or understanding *what* the hell I was doing. But still."

I nodded.

"And you. Gasper. You turned out okay. Better than a lot of our classmates who looked down on you, I'll wager."

"I wonder what happened to those kids from Carver High? The boy who brought us your crutches?"

"Yeah."

After lunch that day, Stevie and I parted amiably. We agreed to stay in touch and he drove back to Big Spring. For weeks after our conversation, I remembered vividly that season of storms, of my mother's headaches and her long days in bed, of mass fears spinning around communists, viruses, Midland's railroad tracks. The whole period seemed to me, now, a giant laboratory experiment testing who would thrive and who would not. Stevie, weak and picked-on—not only had he gained strength through the years, but he had overcome terrible odds. He claimed he'd just been lucky, but I felt he had not given himself enough credit for his steadiness.

I suppose steadiness had seen *me* through, steadiness and hard work. Nothing spectacular. Just regular effort. As a child negotiating the use of crutches, Stevie had had to learn to take one step after another, just as I had had to learn to breathe with even, stoic calm. Perhaps our disadvantages had given us a boost.

And my mother. The severity of her headaches waned as she grew older, but the pain never left her in peace. Its cause—hormonal changes, atmospheric pressures, chemical imbalances, electrical signals in the brain—continued to be debated by the medical establishment, and various remedies were suggested to her over the years, but she just soldiered on, going to bed when she needed to, otherwise doing her business.

She kept dancing, which led to several roles in regional theater, a vast enrichment of her life. Always, my father watched her onstage with proud amazement. As his wistfulness grew, his nostalgia for the past, his discomfort with social change (oh, how he railed against school busing!), he took solace in my mother's achievements. They grew old together gracefully and died within a year of each other, in relative peace, in their eighties.

"We're orphans now," Dee Dee said to me matter-of-factly. In maturity, as in childhood, she'd become a person of no major lows or highs (I say this not to disparage her). She never seemed to want for much and never complained of what she lacked. Achievement and failure have simply never been part of her vocabulary. "Hey, Boob," I'll say to her whenever we meet for lunch. She can take or leave the Petroleum Club, and is just as happy at McDonald's.

In just *getting on* with her life, she may be our community's ideal citizen. Though entrenched in old patterns of thinking (on money, class, and race), the place has nevertheless changed as it needed to, in increments. The Conservation Reserve Program—the federal government's agreement to pay farmers to plant millions of acres with grasses—has kept West Texas free of debilitating dust storms. In *this* instance, the locals have not minded government "interference."

In October 1971, a federal judge in the US District Court for the Western District of Texas ruled that the US Department of Health, Education and Welfare did not have the authority to impose plans for integrating public schools on the Midland Independent School District. The judge said that, in spite of *Brown v. Board of Education*, "in some circumstances schools may remain of one race until new schools can be provided or neighborhood patterns change." He found that, given Midland's housing configurations, the school district was doing all it could do to "meet the constitutional requirements in so far as they relate to Negro children." Further efforts at integration should be left "entirely in the hands of the school board. The Court cannot and would not take over any administrative functions resting in the discretion of school authorities."

Shortly after the judge's pronouncement, busing in town was severely curtailed. Today, Midland's public schools remain largely segregated.

As late as 1986, a mayoral candidate was defeated when his opponent labeled him a "communist."

Still, my father's world, the world in which he'd learned to operate and which, in spite of its contradictions and troubles, he loved, *did* vanish, as he saw it would. I can say from experience that geologists rarely, if ever, drive their sons into the desert now to inspect old wells. From our offices we can sip instant coffee and run remote data checks by computer. To find oil and gas these days we're not even forced to leave our desks. The old rockhounds have gone the way of the beasts that dropped their bones in the ground to power the automated cities and cars that will take us still further from the world my father knew.

As for Raymond "Flyboy" Seaker—naturally, his image lingered with me after my conversation with Stevie. In almost every way, he was this story's most promising figure. A solid family background, graced with intelligence and self-discipline; a driven military man with a spotless service record; a happy, wholesome marriage; a gift with children; and the right job in the right place, admired by his boss, adored by the students he worked with, trusted by their parents. How could the story go so wrong? How could he fly apart so quickly?

It is tempting to blame external forces. Bad luck, malicious intent. The dust storms, whipping up an atmosphere of irritation, swallowing us all; rumors of war, of nuclear accident, of disease, the plane crash over town: they combined, horribly, to be as overwhelming as the sky's brown wall. As we know from myths, from the history of the planet, catastrophe requires *someone* to be held accountable. And Mr. Seaker—well, he was the Chosen One.

But his reaction. *That's* what I return to (I credit my mother for the insight—her example of fortitude). His utter collapse after the death of his brother. His resistance to his wife's pleas that they "make a baby." His resignation from the school, when he felt he'd betrayed the black kids. Taken together, his actions amount to an astounding inflexibility, born perhaps of those same qualities that made him so attractive in the beginning. A sense of honor. Of unwavering duty. Of the need to take charge, as when he stood his ground with the Mexican boys. And when *that* illusion was shattered—the illusion that he *could* control the community's weather—the façade of strength fell with shocking swiftness and finality.

My father with the nail in his foot—even *he*, exposed to me in the shadow of the well as a vulnerable and faltering man . . . even he learned to wobble with change better than Mr. Seaker ever could.

And yet what a figure he had been! Standing on the playground, kind and affable and smiling, his shirt sleeves rolled to his elbows, revealing the sinewy strength of his arms and hands. The embodiment of safety and assurance. It is an image I would like to hold in my mind the way a Grecian urn holds in the core of its fired metals, its sculpted curves, a golden image of eternal love or harmony or bounty. The very best of human experience, human communion. Whenever the school bell rang, releasing us onto the field, propelling us on waves of laughter and energy toward this good man, standing there waiting for us, I felt—we all felt, I know we did—we were going to be all right. Despite the threat of war and dust and change, we saw what we might become, we saw a vision of our future, and we were mightily consoled.

# Biographical Note

Tracy Daugherty is the author of several books of fiction and nonfiction, including the *New York Times* bestseller *The Last Love Song: A Biography of Joan Didion*. His short stories and essays have appeared in the *New Yorker*, *Vanity Fair*, *British Vogue*, the *Paris Review* online, *McSweeney's*, and many other journals. The recipient of fellowships from the Guggenheim Foundation and the National Endowment for the Arts, he lives in Corvallis, Oregon, with his wife, writer Marjorie Sandor.